T
the Swamp

Ahead of him, Winfield gave a hoarse scream. Tallon heard violent splashing sounds and cursed his blind helplessness. He retrieved the eyeset from the thrashing doctor, put it on, and was jolted with green blurs of brilliant light.

When Tallon oriented himself he could see that the doctor was lying on his back, his right leg sunk to the knee in a seething patch of turbulence. Red stains spread on the water, and eight jointed stalks whipped in the air.

Tallon tried to spear the muck spider, but the doctor grabbed the weapon and worked it close to his leg. "I'm getting it," Winfield grunted. He grasped the spear high on its shaft and began to go up it, hand over hand.

Winfield was winning the battle, but there was something he was forgetting. . . .

denotes an Illustrated Book

NIGHTWALK

Bob Shaw

A DELL BOOK

Published by
DELL PUBLISHING CO., INC.
1 Dag Hammarskjold Plaza
New York, New York 10017

ISBN: 0-440-15996-2

Reprinted by arrangement with the author.
Printed in the United States of America
First Dell printing—March 1979

one

A winter night, sharp and frozen, had moved in over New Wittenburg, pressing down hard on the bitter streets, laying uneven swaths of frost on the concrete desert of the space terminal.

Tallon leaned against the window of his room, looking out. The long hours of night lay ahead, and he wondered how he was going to get through. Not even the possibility of passing through the eighty thousand portals that led to Earth could ease his depression. He had dozed on top of the rumpled bedclothes for several hours, and during that time the world seemed to have died. The hotel felt empty.

He lit a cigarette and exhaled a gentle river of smoke that coursed flatly along the glass of the window. Little circular areas of condensation formed on the inside of the glass, centered on droplets that clung to the outside. *Were they going to come for him?* The question was a dull ache that had gnawed at him since he made the pickup a week earlier.

Normally the probability of success would have been high, but this time there were things Tallon did not like. He drew hard on the heady smoke, making the cigarette crackle faintly. It had been lousy luck, McNulty having a heart attack just when he did; but it had also been an error on the part of someone back in the Block. What in hell were they doing, putting a man into the field without making absolutely certain he couldn't get sick? McNulty had panicked after his attack and had made an unorthodox transfer that still shocked Tallon every time he remembered its clumsiness. He ground the cigarette under his shoe and swore to make somebody pay for the mistake when he got back to the Block. If he got back to the Block.

By a conscious effort he denied himself another cigarette. The room seemed to have grown smaller in the week he had stayed there. Hotels on Emm Luther were on the bottom of the scale as far as comfort and amenities went. His room was not inexpensive, yet it contained nothing but a bed with a smudged headboard, and a few shabby pieces of furniture. A cobweb waved forlornly from the warm air vent. The walls were a kind of bureaucrat green—the color of despair.

Sucking in air through his teeth in a hiss of disgust, Tallon returned to the window and leaned his forehead on the chill glass. He looked out across the throbbing lights of the alien city, noting the subtle effect of the higher gravity in the architecture of the towers and spires—a reminder that he was far from home.

Eighty thousand portals there were between here and Earth, representing uncountable millions of light-years; curtains of star systems, layer upon layer of them, made it impossible to pick out even the loose cluster of which Sol was a part. Too far; much too far. Loyalties were stretched too thin over those distances. Earth, the need for new portals, the Block—at this distance, what did it all mean?

Tallon suddenly realized he was hungry. He switched on a light and examined himself in the room's single mirror. His straight black hair was slightly untidy. The long, rather serious face—which might have been that of an accountant or a jazz player with a leaning toward theory—was shaded with stubble, but he decided it was unlikely to attract attention. Momentarily and childishly pleased at the thought of eating, he ran a comb through his hair, turned off the light, and opened the door.

He was stepping out into the corridor when the first smell of danger came to him. The hotel was quiet. And now that he thought of it, no vehicle had passed along the normally busy street below his window during the whole time he had stood there.

Snuffling with panic, wiping his upper lip with the back of his hand, Tallon went back into his room and edged the window open a little. The unsteady murmur of city traffic billowed into the room on the cold air; and yet nothing was moving in the one thoroughfare immediately below. Would they go to all that trouble? He pulled his jaw sideways, frowning in thought, then realized he was deceiving himself by simulating doubt. For what he had in his memory they would seal off the city, the continent, the whole planet of Emm Luther.

It's happening to me, he thought, but a wave of irritation submerged his fear. Why did everybody have to stick so carefully to the rules? Why was it that if somebody on your side made a mistake, somebody on their side always

6

chopped you for it? Were they not going to make an exception, even for Sam Tallon, the center of the universe?

Moving with sudden feverish speed, he locked the door and dragged his suitcase out of the closet. There was something that should have been done earlier, and his forehead prickled at the thought of the risk he had taken by delaying so long. He took his old-style transistor radio from the case, removed its battery, and went to the mirror. Ducking his head slightly, Tallon parted the hair on his left temple and worked through it until he had isolated two silver strands. He raised the battery to his forehead, and after a moment's hesitation, pressed the gleaming strands to its terminals.

Eyes opaque with pain, rocking slightly on his feet, Tallon slowly and clearly recited the information. It took only a few seconds for him to go through the four groups of digits. When he had finished he reversed the battery and, with a longer hesitation, made the connection again. This time it really hurt as the pea-sized capsule implanted in his brain snapped itself shut, imprisoning a fragment of the living tissue.

He put the battery back in the radio, found the metallic hairs again, and jerked them from his scalp. Tallon smiled wryly. It had been easier than he had expected. The Lutherians usually avoided killing people, partly because it was the planetary government's official creed, but mainly because their knowledge of hypnotic techniques had advanced far enough to make it unnecessary. If he was taken, the first thing they would do would be to use a brain-brush on him to wipe out what he had learned. But now it would fail. Even if he were to be killed, the Block would find a sorrowing relative to apply for the return of his body to Earth, and the pea-sized fragment of his brain would still be alive in its beautifully engineered cocoon. The Block woud be able to extract what it wanted to know.

Tallon wondered coolly if, in spite of all the assurances, a tiny frightened ghost of his own personality would still be there in that dark little cell—alive and screaming when the electrodes came blindly probing. I'm getting too pessimistic, he thought. It must be an occupational disease. Who says I'm going to die?

He took the flat, high-velocity automatic from his pocket and weighed it in his hand. The Block would expect him to use it, even though Earth and Emm Luther were not officially at war. When the capsule had been im-

7

planted in his head there had been an unwritten, unspoken clause in the agreement. With the information locked up tight, preserved independent of his own life, the Block would rather he got himself killed and shipped back home than be locked safely away in an escape-proof prison. Nobody had even hinted at the clause—he would have quite on the spot if they had; but it was there just the same. And the best way to get killed would be to start shooting at members of the E.L.S.P. Tallon unloaded the automatic, threw it in a drawer, and dropped the clip into the wastebasket.

The strings of digits he had memorized were the coordinates of the new portal, plus the jump bearing and jump increment involved, which the luck of the galactic draw had awarded to Emm Luther rather than to Earth. They represented nothing less than one brand-new Earth-type planet. He, Sam Tallon, was the possessor of perhaps the most important single secret in the universe. But he was not going to die for it—not for anything or anybody. All he owed the Block was a reasonable attempt at escaping. He lit a fresh cigarette and sat on the edge of the bed.

Somewhere in the city of New Wittenburg there was a specialist whose name and address Tallon did not know. The specialist would contact him when it was safe. His job was to administer the drug pack, the treatment, which by both physical and psychosomatic means would alter Tallon's appearance sufficiently to get him through the checkpoints at the space terminal. His skin, hair, and eye pigmentation would be changed; the fingerprint patterns would be altered; even his Bertillon measurements would be changed—by drugs that produced tensions and contractions in the body's musculature and connective tissues.

Tallon had never had the treatment before and was unhappy at the prospect, but it would be better than sinking out of sight in a Lutherian prison. If only he could leave the hotel and stay on the loose, the specialist would find him. The problem was how to get out.

He pulled deeply on his cigarette, almost allowed the smoke to escape from his mouth, then drew it back into his lungs. The excess made him dizzy. He lay back on his elbows and tried to assess his chances objectively.

With full equipment there would have been six possible ways to leave his room—the door and window, the two other walls, and the floor and ceiling—but, thanks to McNulty, he had been forced to travel without gear. The E.L.S.P. did not know that, though, which was why they had gone to the trouble of englobing him. He guessed they

8

were at that minute covering the street outside, the corridor, and the rooms above, below, and on each side.

Apart from the useless automatic, he had nothing but a pair of thrust shoes in extremely doubtful condition. Assuming the others really were out there and not just a product of his nerves, the situation was about as hopeless as they come. The only course offering any hope at all was, as he had originally intended, to walk as calmly as possible toward the restaurant. A window at the end of the corridor looked out on a different street. If he got to that, there might be a slight chance.

But this time the door to the corridor refused to open.

Tallon twisted the handle violently and pulled with all his strength, then remembered the Block had warned him not to exert himself too much for a few hours after triggering the capsule in his head. He relaxed and backed away from the door, half expecting it to be blasted open at any second. He was caught. The only question still remaining was which of the three E.L.S.P. network executives was handling the operation. The ban on straightforward liquidation, imposed by the rigid semitheocracy that prevailed on Emm Luther, had led them to develop idiosyncratic ways of handling politically dangerous prisoners. The cardex in Tallon's memory flicked over, unbidden, turning up their names and a summary of what was likely to happen to him "accidentally while resisting arrest."

There was Kreuger, who liked to immobilize his captives by cutting their Achilles tendons; there was Cherkassky, who filled them so full of psychoneuro drugs that they never again had a peaceful night's sleep; and finally there was Zepperitz. Zepperitz and his methods made the other two men seem almost benign.

Suddenly appalled by his own stupidity at ever having allowed himself to be drawn into the intelligence game, Tallon drew a chair into the center of the room and sat on it. He interlocked his hands behind his back—a neat, passive bundle—and waited. The destruction of Tallon as a political being, begun the first time he had failed to find a recognizable constellation in Emm Luther's night sky, was complete.

He felt cold, apprehensive, and impossibly ill.

two

There are roughly eighty thousand portals between Emm Luther and Earth. To make the journey home you must pass through all of them, regardless of how afraid you become, regardless of how far you feel body outstripping soul during the flicker-transits across the distant reaches of the Rim.

Your ship reaches the first portal by diagonally breasting the galactic drift for almost five days. The portal is relatively close to Emm Luther at present, but they are separating from each other at a rate of some four miles a second. This is because the planet and its parent sun are swimming with the galactic tide, whereas the portal is an imaginary sphere anchored to a point in the immovable topography of null-space.

If your ship carries good astrogation equipment it may enter the portal at speed; but should the computers in control have any doubt at all about their exact location, they may spend days discarding velocity and maneuvering for position. They know—and you, sweating in your G-cell, know too—that if the ship is not safely inside the portal when the jump takes place its passengers will never again breathe the soft thick air of Earth. The alien geometry of null-space will take care of that.

As you wait, with dry throat and icy forehead, for the relays to strike you pray that some crazy fluke won't cast you up innumerable hopeless light-years from home. But this is human emotion at work.

Null-space is incomprehensible, but it is not irrational. Provided every glass and metal organ in the guts of your ship is functioning properly, you could make a million jumps from A through null-space to B without the slightest mishap. The difficulties arise because null-space is not reciprocal. Having reached B, the same jump in the opposite direction will not return you to A; in fact, it will take you to any random point in the universe except A. Once that has happened there is nothing for it but to go on making more and more random leaps. If you keep it up long enough and are extremely lucky, you may emerge

10

within reach of a habitable world, but the odds are not good.

In the first century of interstellar exploration Earth alone dispatched some forty million robot probes, of which less than two hundred chanced to make their way back. Of that number, exactly eight had found usable planetary systems. Not one of the handful of manned ships that accidentally made open-ended jumps was ever seen again—on Earth, anyway. Some of them may still be going, carrying the descendants of their original crews, cosmic Flying Dutchmen glimpsed only by uncomprehending stars as their destiny of flicker-transits gradually takes them beyond the reach of human thought.

The eight successful probes of that first century established zigzagging trade lanes, which the manned ships that came afterward were very careful to follow closely. That is the other aspect of null-space travel that troubles you as you wait for the relays to act. Although it was a logical deduction from the absence of reciprocity in null-space, a few pioneers discovered the hard way that jumping from a point near A will not take you to a corresponding point near B. Get more than about two light-seconds from the established jumping-off point, the so-called portal, and you are off on your own random pilgrimage to the far side of eternity.

That is why, during the final slow seconds as you float in your G-cell and breathe the rubber-smelling air, you pray and you sweat.

That is also why the planet Emm Luther, formerly a colony of Earth and now autonomous, jealously guarded the few strings of figures locked in Sam Tallon's brain. Emm Luther had only a single continent, and her devouring need for new breathing space equaled that of Earth itself. She had one incredible stroke of luck in a probe that found a green planet only four hundred portals out and less than two thousand back.

All she needed was time to consolidate her hold there before the big ships—the invincible sperm of Earth's ceaseless self-multiplication—could storm the new and fertile womb.

three

Tallon did not have long to wait.

His first realization that he was under attack came when he found himself dancing with Myra, a girl who had died back on Earth twenty years earlier.

No, he whispered, *I don't want this.* But she was there in his arms as they slowly gyrated in the varicolored dimness of the Stardust Room. He tried to feel the hard pressure of the chair in the dingy hotel room on Emm Luther, but the effort seemed pointless, for that was part of a future which was still a long way off.

Suddenly he was very much younger, still working for his degree in electronics, and he was holding Myra. It was all *real*. His eyes filled gratefully with the sight of her massive helmet of auburn hair, her whiskey-colored eyes. They moved slowly and contentedly to the sound of the music, with Myra, as always, a fraction behind the beat. She never could dance very well, he thought warmly, but there would be lots of time to work on it after they were married. In the meantime it was enough to drift on and on through pastel mists and star-shot twilight.

The ballroom tilted ponderously away. Another time, another place. He was sitting in the comfortable old bar of the Berkeley, waiting for her. Oases of orange light reflecting on paneled walls of rich dark wood. She was taking far too long, and he grew angry. Myra knew where he was waiting, so if she couldn't keep the date she could at least ring him. Probably starting to take too much for granted, expecting him to go all the way out to her place to see what was wrong. Well, he would teach her a lesson. He began to drink determinedly, vindictively—and the horror was growing, spreading like a dark stain in spite of his frantic efforts to stop it.

Next morning. The drowsy quietness of the standards lab. The newspaper spread on the cigarette-scarred bench and, incredibly, Myra's face looking up at him from the matte plastic sheets. Her father, a sad, mumbling giant who had been deserted years before by Myra's mother,

12

had smothered Myra with a pillow, then opened his wrists with a portable circular saw.

Dissolving colors, the searching tides of grief, again the music, and they were dancing; but this time Myra was dragging far behind the slow rhythms. She was limp and heavy. He fought to hold her up, and her breath sobbed and gurgled in his ear. . . .

Tallon screamed and clamped his fingers on the greasy arms of the chair.

"Here he comes," a voice said. "Romantic little fellow, isn't he? You never can tell just by looking at them." Somebody laughed quietly.

Tallon opened his eyes. The room was filled with men in the gray whipcords of the E.L.S.P. civil security force. They carried small arms, most of them with the fan-shaped snouts of hornet guns, but he noticed several circular muzzles belonging to a more traditional type of weapon. Their faces were amused, derisive, some of them still indented with faint pink lines left by the masks that had protected them from the psychoneuro gas.

His stomach was erupting noisily at every breath, but Tallon found the physical nausea unimportant compared with the emotional turmoil still rocking his senses. The psychic shock was mingled with an intolerable feeling of outrage, of having been invaded, slit open, and pinned to a dissecting board like a laboratory specimen. *Myra, my love . . . I'm sorry.* Oh, you bastards, you grinning, stinking——

He tensed for a moment, ready to dive forward, then realized he was reacting exactly as expected. This was why they had used an LSD derivative instead of a simple knockout gas. Tallon made himself relax; he could take anything Kreuger, Cherkassky, or Zepperitz could hand out, and he would prove it. He would live on, in one reasonably healthy piece, even if it was only to read every book in some prison library.

"Very good, Tallon," a voice said. "Self-control is so important in your profession." The speaker moved into Tallon's line of vision. He was a dry, thin-faced man, wearing the black coat and white dog collar of an Emm Lutherian government official. Tallon recognized the narrow face, the vertically wrinkled neck, and the incongruously lush wavy hair of Lorin Cherkassky, number two man in the security executive's hierarchy.

Tallon nodded impassively. "Good evening. I wondered——"

"Just keep it shut," interrupted a chunky-shouldered blond who wore sergeant's chevrons.

"It's all right, Sergeant." Cherkassky waved the younger man aside. "We mustn't discourage Mr. Tallon from being communicative. He may be expected to tell us quite a lot during the next few days."

"I'll be glad to tell you all I know, of course," Tallon said quickly. "What's the point of trying to hold on to it?"

"Precisely!" Cherkassky's voice was an excited yelp, reminding Tallon of the little man's notorious instability. "What's the point? I'm glad you see it that way. Now, Mr. Tallon, will you answer one question right away?"

"What is it? Yes."

Cherkassky walked to the chest of drawers, his head making peacocklike movements on the long neck at every step, and took out the empty automatic pistol. "Where is the ammunition for this weapon?"

"In there. I threw it in the wastebasket."

"I see," Cherkassky said, stooping to retrieve the clip. "You hid it in the wastebasket."

Tallon shifted uneasily on the seat. This was too childish to be true. "I dropped it in the wastebasket. I didn't want it. I didn't want any trouble." He kept his voice low and flat.

Cherkassky nodded sympathetically. "That's what I would say if I were in your position. Yes, that's about the best thing you could say." He slid the clip into the pistol butt and handed it to the sergeant. "Don't lose this, Sergeant. It's evidence."

Tallon opened his mouth to speak, then closed it abruptly. The very childishness of the proceedings was an important part of the technique. There is nothing more galling, more frustrating, than being forced to act like an adult when everybody around you is behaving like a malicious juvenile. But he was going to take it all, without cracking.

There was a long silence during which Cherkassky watched him intently. Tallon sat perfectly motionless, trying to subdue occasional gusts of brilliant memory shards, pictures of Myra still alive, pale skin, whiskey-colored eyes. He became aware of the seat cutting into the backs of his legs and wondered if any movement on his part would bring the multiple impact of a hornet gun. Most authorities regarded it as a humane weapon, but Tallon had once accidentally stopped a full charge of the tiny

14

drug-laden darts, and the ensuing paralysis had caused thirty minutes of agony.

As the silence stretched into minutes, without any preparations being made to remove him from the hotel, Tallon began to worry. He looked around the room, trying to find a clue, but the faces of the E.L.S.P. men remained professionally impassive. Cherkassky pottered around contentedly, smiling and shrinking back against the wall each time he met Tallon's eyes.

Tallon became aware of a peculiar sensation involving the skin of his forehead and cheeks, an icy feeling combined with waves of pinpricks passing across the individual pores. I've graduated, he thought; I'm having my first cold sweat.

Seconds later the door was bumped open, and a uniformed man came in carrying a heavy box of gray metal. He set it on a chair, glanced briefly at Tallon, and left. Cherkassky snapped his fingers, and the blond sergeant opened the box, revealing a control panel and coiled leads on plastic reels. In a shallow tray, the ten circular terminals of a brain-brush headset gleamed like tawdry jewelry.

"Now, Tallon—time for a little editing." Cherkassky's powdery face had become businesslike.

"Here? In the hotel?"

"Why not? The longer you have the information in your head, the greater chance you have of transferring it to someone else."

"But it takes a trained psychologist to isolate any specific sequence of thoughts," Tallon protested. "You're likely to blot out whole areas of my memory that have nothing to—" He stopped as Cherkassky's head began to make little self-satisfied swaying movements on the turkey neck. Tallon swore silently at himself. He had intended to take it all without a word, absorb anything they could hand out—but he had begun to squeal before they had even touched him. So much for the short and spectacular career of Iron Man Tallon. He compressed his lips and sat staring straight ahead as Cherkassky positioned the linked terminals on his head. The sergeant gave a signal, and the encircling wall of gray uniforms retreated into the corridor, making the room suddenly bigger and colder. In the dismal light the single cobweb still waved inanely from the warm-air vent.

Cherkassky stood beside the chair that held the gray box, stooping slightly to make adjustments on the verniers.

He ran his eyes over the dials and glanced up at Tallon's face.

"Did you know, Tallon, that your basal resistance is abnormally low? Perhaps you perspire easily; that always lowers the skin resistance. You aren't a sweaty person, are you?" Cherkassky's nose wrinkled in distaste, and the sergeant chuckled quietly.

Tallon scowled past him toward the window. It had misted over during the time the room was crowded, and the few city lights that were visible looked like balls of illuminated cotton. He longed to be outside, breathing the sharp starry air. Myra had liked walking on frosty nights....

"Mr. Tallon wants us to stop wasting time," Cherkassky said severely. "He's right, of course. Let's get down to business. Now, Tallon, just so that there are absolutely no misconceptions on either side—you are in your present predicament because you are part of an intelligence network that by pure chance obtained details of portal coordinates, jump increment, and jump bearings of the planet Aitch Mühlenberg, a territorial acquisition of the revered government of Emm Luther. The information was transferred to you, and you have committed it to memory. Correct?"

Tallon nodded compliantly, wondering if the brain-brush would be as unpleasant as the capsule. Cherkassky picked up the remote control and poised his thumb over the red button. It dawned on Tallon that the instrument being used on him was a standard model, the same model as used by less reputable psychiatrists. He began to wonder just how unofficial his present treatment was. On Emm Luther, with its single continent run by a single world government, there had never been any need to develop the huge, highly organized intelligence and counterespionage agencies that still proliferated on Earth. For this reason the three Lutherian network executives were given an almost free hand, like contractors on any normal government undertaking, but they were answerable to the Temporal Moderator, the planet's equivalent of a president. The question was, how far was a man like Cherkassky allowed to indulge his own idiosyncrasies?

"All right, then," Cherkassky said. "We want you to focus your thoughts on the information. Try to get it nice and clean. And don't try to fool us by thinking about something else; we will be checking. I will raise my hand when I'm going to erase, which will be about five seconds from now."

Tallon worked to marshal the strings of figures, all at

16

once desperately afraid of losing his own name. Cherkassky's hand made a preliminary movement, and Tallon fought down his panic as the figures refused to flow properly, even with his Block-trained memory, then . . . nothing. The numerals that would have given Earth a whole new world were gone. There had been no pain, no sound, no sensation of any kind, but the vital fragment of knowledge was no longer his. As the expectation of pain faded Tallon relaxed a little.

"That wasn't too horrible, was it?" Cherkassky smoothed the thick crown of glossy hair, which seemed to thrive like a parasite at the expense of his frail, dry body. "Quite painless, I'm told."

"I didn't feel anything," Tallon conceded.

"But the information has been erased?"

"Yes. It's gone."

"Astonishing!" Cherkassky's voice became conversational. "I never fail to be astonished at what this little box of tricks can do. You know, it makes libraries unnecessary. All anyone has to do is get one book he really likes, then he can go on reading and erasing, reading and erasing for the rest of his life."

"It's an idea," Tallon said suspiciously. "Do you mind if I take this thing off now?"

"Don't even twitch your toes until Mr. Cherkassky gives the word." The blond sergeant tapped Tallon on the shoulder with his hornet gun.

"Oh, come on now, Sergeant," Cherkassky protested amiably. "You mustn't be too hard on him. After all, he has been very cooperative. Very communicative, too. I mean, look how much he told earlier about that girl he knew back on Earth. Most men keep that sort of stuff to themselves. What was her name, Tallon? Ah, I remember— Mary."

"Myra," Tallon corrected automatically, then noticed the broadening smile on the sergeant's face.

Cherkassky's thumb had come down on the red button.

Tallon stared up into his thin, strangely triumphant face with an overwhelming feeling of having been robbed. Something, some part of him was gone. But what? He tried to explore his own mind, looking for dark gaps in his memory. There was nothing but a lingering sense of loss.

Anger came fountaining up through him then, clean and pure. Tallon felt it burn away all caution and common sense, and was grateful.

17

"You're filth, Cherkassky," he said quietly. "You're a disease."

The muzzle of the hornet gun came down on his shoulder, viciously, and at the same time he saw Cherkassky's thumb go for the button again. Tallon tried to throw an unwanted scrap of thought up into the forefront of his mind before the contact was made. *The brittle-star is a marine animal related to the*—Blank!

Cherkassky backed away from Tallon, mouth twitching violently, thumb poised over the button. This can go on all night, Tallon thought. By morning I'll be as good as dead, because Sam Tallon is the total of all his remembered experiences and Cherkassky is going to whittle them down to nothing.

"Go ahead, Lorie," the sergeant said. "Give him another jab. Keep at him."

"I will, Sergeant, I will; but it has to be done systematically." Cherkassky had backed almost to the window, stretching the control cable to its limit. The street, Tallon remembered, was seven stories down. Not very far, but far enough.

He drove forward out of the chair, his suddenly heightened senses clearly distinguishing the sound of the chair falling, the satisfying crunch of his head into Cherkassky's face, the angry whine of the hornet gun, the splintering impact as the window gave way ... then they were out in the cold, black air, with the street lights blossoming below.

Cherkassky's body went rigid in Tallon's arms, and he screamed as they fell. Tallon fought to gain an upright position, but the higher gravity of Emm Luther was giving him very little time. He let go of Cherkassky, but Cherkassky's arms were locked around Tallon's chest like steel straps. Moaning with panic, Tallon twisted until his legs were below him. The thrust shoes, triggered automatically by the proximity of the ground, reacted forcefully. As his knees buckled under the deceleration Tallon felt Cherkassky's grip tear loose, and the little man went on down, thrashing like a hooked fish. Tallon heard the impact of his body on the footpath.

He landed on the concrete beside Cherkassky's crumpled body, the thrust of the antigrav soles increasing by inverse squares until the moment of contact. Cherkassky was still alive; that much of the plan had gone wrong. But at least Tallon was out in the open again. He turned to run and found the lead of the brain-brush dangling from the headset, which was still clinging to his scalp.

In the act of snatching it off he noticed the movement of gray uniforms in the doorways of the shopping center across the empty street. Whistles shrilled at both ends of the block. A fraction of a second later he heard the hornet guns in action, and then he was caught in a whining cloud of darts, which made a rapid *thock-thock-thock* as they stitched his clothes to his body.

Tallon reeled and went down, helpless.

He lay on his back, paralyzed, and found a moment of strange peace. The E.L.S.P. men were still blasting away zealously with their hornet guns, but lying down he made a poor target for the horizontal swarms of darts, and they were not getting to him. The stars, even in their unfamiliar constellations, looked good. Up there were other men who, provided they had courage enough to stand the random galaxy-wide pattern of flicker-transits spreading their souls thin across the universe, were free to travel. Sam Tallon could no longer take part in that awesome commerce, but he would never be completely a prisoner while he could look into the night skies.

The hornet guns abruptly ceased firing. Tallon listened for the sound of running feet, but instead heard a movement unexpectedly close by.

A figure moved into his field of view and, incredibly, it was Cherkassky. His face was a voodoo mask of flayed skin and blood, and one arm hung awkwardly at his side. He moved his good hand forward painfully, and Tallon saw that it held a hornet gun.

"No man," Cherkassky whispered, "no man has ever ..." He fired the gun at point-blank range.

Hornet guns were regarded as a humane weapon, and usually they did no lasting damage, but Cherkassky was a professional. Tallon, completely immobilized by the drugs, could not even blink as the darts ripped viciously into his eyes, robbing him forever of light and beauty and stars.

four

For Tallon there was no pain; that would come only when the paralysis drug began to be absorbed by his system. At first he was not even sure of what had happened, for darkness did not come at once. Instead, his distorted view of Cherkassky and the wavering gun muzzle was replaced by an incoherent universe of light—splintering flashes, marching geometric patterns of color, pine-tree shapes of amethyst and pink.

But there was no escaping the processes of logic. A hornet-gun charge from a distance of twelve inches . . .

My eyes must be gone!

Tallon had time for a moment of anguish; then all his consciousness contracted to focus on a new phenomenon: he was unable to breathe. With all physical sensation blanketed by the drug, he had no way of knowing why his breath had been shut off; but it was not too difficult to guess. Blinding him had been only the first installment; now Cherkassky was out to finish the job. Tallon discovered he was not very afraid, considering what was happening, perhaps because the ancient reaction of panic—the downward, air-seeking thrust of the diaphragm—was blocked by his paralysis. If only he had kicked in Cherkassky's head while he had the chance.

There was the sound of running feet drawing near, then voices:

"Corporal! Lift Mr. Cherkassky to the car. It looks like he's seriously injured."

"Right, Sarge."

The second voice was followed by the sound of boots scuffing on the concrete, and Tallon suddenly gulped air. Cherkassky must have passed out and fallen across his face. Tallon accepted the air gratefully; then he heard voices again.

"Sarge! Look at the Earther's eyes. Can a hornet gun do *that*?"

"You want me to show you? Get Mr. Cherkassky into the car, then shove the Earther in the tender."

20

Vague shifts in his sense of balance told Tallon the orders were being carried out. Whistles sounded; vehicle turbines were spun up noisily. And indeterminate time went by; then Tallon began to feel pain. . . .

Less than twenty-four hours had passed, but already Tallon thought he could feel the quickening of the other senses that accompanies the loss of sight.

In the police headquarters in New Wittenburg somebody had jabbed a hypodermic into his neck, and he had regained consciousness with the comforting feeling of bandages across his face. He had been given a hot drink and escorted to a bed—all without having a word addressed to him—and, miraculously, had slept. While he was sleeping someone had removed his shoes and replaced them with thin-soled boots several sizes too large for him.

Now he was being transported in another vehicle, accompanied by three or four anonymous E.L.S.P. officers, who communicated with him by occasional pushes and nudges. Tallon was too helpless to try to get them to talk to him. His mind was unable to encompass anything but the fact that he was unable to see.

The vehicle slowed down, heeled twice as it turned corners, then stopped. When Tallon was helped out he knew with certainty he was on an airfield. He felt the random slap of air currents, which spoke of open space, and smelled aviation fuel; then, in confirmation, he heard the sound of huge turbines winding up near by.

Tallon felt a faint flicker of interest. He had never flown on Emm Luther because it was expensive, and traveling this way would have made him too conspicuous. The civil aircraft were large, but carried comparatively small payloads owing to governmental regulations controlling their design. The fuselages were heavily armored, and the wings were inefficient by Earth standards, because they carried the complete power, fuel, and control systems. In the event of a crash landing the wings, with their deadly fuel load, were shed by explosive bolts. The planetary government had made flying safe on Emm Luther, regardless of economics, and in that respect had earned Tallon's reluctant approval. He wished the Temporal Moderator would display such good sense in the staffing of governmental agencies.

Unseen hands helped him up steps into the warm, plastic-smelling interior of the plane and into a seat. Other hands fastened the safety webbing, and suddenly he was left alone. Tallon listened intently, using his newly discovered trick of consciously seeking different sound frequencies, but the only voices he picked up were those of the E.L.S.P. men conversing in whispers. Evidently they had laid on a special flight just for him. Feeling cold, Tallon slumped down in his seat and wished he could at least look through the windows.

His eyes no longer hurt, but the outraged nerves were still throwing up pseudo images, some of which were painfully brilliant flashes of color. Tallon wondered how long it would be before they gave him proper medical attention. It was not until he heard the *whump* of the door closing, followed by an increase in engine pitch, that he wondered where he was being taken. There was, he decided, only one real possibility: the Pavilion.

The prison reserved for political enemies of Emm Luther was on the southernmost tip of the single continent. It had originally been the winter residence of the first Temporal Moderator, who had intended to fill in the marshy region that joined the rocky islet to the mainland. But he had changed his mind and moved north instead. In those early days of colonization when construction materials were still scarce, some unknown civil servant had seen the possibilities of the Pavilion as an escape-proof prison. Several well-placed cutting charges had broken the spine of the little peninsula, allowing the warm waters of the Erfurt Sea to lap across it. Within a few years the original marshy area had become a superswamp that could be crossed only by air.

The Pavilion held fewer prisoners now than in the years when the present political overlords were emerging. And it had confirmed the civil servant's foresight: Nobody had ever escaped from it.

After an extremely smooth takeoff and a short climb the aircraft settled in its course, with near-silent engines; only an occasional slipping sensation let Tallon know he was moving through the sky. He sat listening to the whisper of air and the infrequent whine of control servos, then drifted into an uneasy sleep.

He awoke to the sound of the engines in full throat, the big jets hammering fierce vibrations through the plane's structure. Tallon gripped the armrests of his seat. A few agonizing seconds went by in his private night-world before he realized what was happening: The big aircraft was making a vertical landing. At Emm Luther's gravity this maneuver involved such a prodigious expenditure of fuel that it would only be done either in an emergency or in a landing where there was no room for even a primitive airstrip. Tallon decided they had arrived at the Pavilion.

Coming down the steps from the passenger door, Tallon's first impression was of the warmth of the air in contrast to the bitter winds of the New Wittenburg winter. He had forgotten that the thousand-mile flight would bring him close to the planet's tropics. As he was being guided across an area of rippled concrete, with heat coming through the soles of his thin boots, Tallon sensed the nearness of the sea with a sudden stab of anguish. He had always liked looking at the sea. He was led through a doorway and along a succession of echoing corridors, then finally into a quiet room, where he was pushed into a chair. The booted feet withdrew. Wondering if he was alone, Tallon turned his head from side to side, aware of his utter helplessness.

"Well, Tallon, this is just about the end of the line for you. I guess you'll be glad to rest for a while." The voice was deep and strong. Tallon visualized its owner as a big man of about fifty. The important thing was that he had been spoken to personally, and not unkindly. Another human mind was reaching out through the darkness. He opened his mouth to reply, but his throat felt tight. He nodded his head, feeling like a schoolboy.

"Don't worry, Tallon. The reaction is catching up with you. I'll see you get something to help you over the next few days. I'm Dr. Muller, head of the psychology department attached to the prison. I'm going to give you a routine check to make sure that you-know-what has been permanently erased from your memory; then I'm going to hand you over to my colleague, Dr. Heck, who'll see what he can do about your eyes."

"My eyes!" Tallon felt an irrational surge of hope. "Do you mean ... ?"

"That's not my department, Tallon. Dr. Heck will examine you as soon as I'm finished, and I'm sure he'll do everything that can be done."

Absorbed with the idea that perhaps his eyes were not so badly damaged as he had imagined, Tallon sat patiently through the testing procedures, which took nearly an hour. The program involved more than a dozen tiny injections, some of which brought on sharp attacks of nausea and dizziness. Questions were thrown at him continually, often in women's voices, although he had heard nobody else enter the room. Sometimes the interrogative voices seemed to be originating right inside his head— persuasive, seductive, or frightening in turn, and always irresistible. Tallon heard his own voice gasping out incoherent replies. Finally he felt the terminals being stripped from his head and body.

"That appears to be that, Tallon," Dr. Muller said. "As far as I'm concerned, you're clear. I'm going to certify you as a normal class-three security risk, which means you'll join the other detainees and will have all the customary privileges. In a way, you're lucky."

"I take it you use the word in a very loose sense, Doctor." Tallon fingered the bandages over his eyes. "Or do you mean lucky in comparison with some of the others Cherkassky has brought in here?"

"I mean, considering the sort of information you had, any other government in the universe, including that of Earth, would have executed you immediately."

"Cherkassky tried to execute my mind. Do you know he kept on pressing the red button on that——"

"Enough!" Muller's voice had lost its friendliness. "That isn't my department."

"My mistake, Doctor. I thought you said you were head of psychology. Or is it that you don't want to think too much about the kind of men you work for?"

There was a long silence. When Muller spoke again he had regained his professional warmth. "I'm prescribing something to get you through the backlash period, Tallon. I'm sure you'll find you'll settle down here very well. Now Dr. Heck will see you."

Muller must have given a signal of some kind, for a door opened quietly and Tallon felt a hand grasp his arm. He was led out of the room and along more corridors. The medical block, if that's what it was, seemed a lot bigger than he had expected. Although lagging behind Earth in many fields of research, it was possible that Emm Luther could be advanced in surgical techniques. After all, Tallon thought, this is the twenty-second century. There are all kinds of things that can be done for an injured person—microsurgery, cell regeneration, electron surgery, tissue welding.

By the time he was escorted into a room that smelled of antiseptics, Tallon was drenched with perspiration and shaking uncontrollably. Someone guided him to what felt like a high couch and made him lie down. A feeling of warmth on his forehead and lips told him that powerful lights were shining on his face. There was a short delay during which he heard soft footsteps and the rustle of clothing near by. He fought to check the trembling, but it was impossible; the single breath of hope had shattered his control.

"Well now, Mr. Tallon." The man's voice had the slight German accent common on Emm Luther. "You're nervous, I see. Dr. Muller said you'd be in need of medication. I think we'll give you a couple of cc's of one of our blends of distilled tranquility."

"I don't need it," Tallon said determinedly. "If it's all right with you, I'd just like to get on with the . . . with the . . ."

"I understand. Let's see now."

Tallon felt the bandages being gently cut away from his eyes; and then, incredibly, Dr. Heck began to whistle.

"Oh, yes, I see . . . I see. An unfortunate accident, of course, but things could have been worse, Mr. Tallon. I think we can fix this up for you without too much difficulty. It will take a week or so, but we'll be able to patch you up all right."

"Do you mean it?" Tallon drew in an ecstatic, shuddering breath. "Do you really mean you'll be able to do something with my eyes?"

"Of course. We'll start work on the eyelids in the morning—that's the trickiest part—and we'll clean up the bridge of the nose and do something about the brows."

"But my eyes—what about my eyes?"

"No problem. What color would you like?"

"Color?" Tallon felt a chill of fear.

"Yes," Heck said cheerfully. "It's small recompense for being blind, but we can give you a really beautiful pair of brown plastic eyes. Or you can have blue—but with your coloring I wouldn't recommend it."

Tallon made no reply. An icy eternity went by before he felt the welcome needle slide into his arm.

five

The daily routine at the Pavilion, as explained to Tallon, was a simple one—simpler for him than for the other prisoners, for he was excused from all activities except the three daily prayer sessions. As far as he could tell, the Pavilion was more like an army training camp than a prison. The inmates worked seven hours a day at a variety of menial jobs, with a minimum of regimentation, and had a library and sports facilities. In a way it was quite a pleasant place to be, except that there was only one sentence—life.

Taken to the exercise ground on his first day out of the medical block, Tallon settled on the ground with his back to a sun-warmed wall. It was a calm morning, with almost no breeze, and the prison yard was filled with overlapping layers of sound—footsteps, voices, and other noises still to be identified—and beyond them, the audible movement of the sea. Tallon leaned his head back on the warm stones and tried to make himself comfortable.

"You're on your own now, Tallon," the guard said. "The others will show you where everything is. Have fun."

"How can I miss?"

The guard laughed sardonically and moved away. His footsteps had barely faded when Tallon felt something flick lightly against his outstretched leg. He froze, trying to remember if the southern part of the continent had any particularly unpleasant insects.

"Excuse me, sir. You are Mr. Sam Tallon?" The voice carried with it the image of a white-haired, red-faced, backwoods politician.

"That's right." Tallon brushed uneasily at his leg, but felt nothing unusual. "Sam Tallon."

"A great pleasure to meet you, Sam." The newcomer sat down beside Tallon, grunting fiercely in the process. "I'm Logan Winfield. You're quite a hero here in the Pavilion, you know."

"I didn't know."

"Oh, yes. None of us here have any great regard for Mr.

Lorin Cherkassky," Winfield boomed, "but neither had we the enterprise to send him into hospital for an extended stay."

"I wasn't trying to hospitalize him. I meant to kill him."

"A laudable ambition, son. What a pity you didn't succeed. However, your endeavor has made every man in the prison your friend for life; that's how long you're in for, I take it."

"I guess so."

"You guess correctly, son. One of the great benefits of mixing Lutheranism, of the variety we have here, with government is that it simplifies the procedure for dealing with *politicos*. The theory appears to be that as we have cheerfully condemned ourselves to everlasting torment in the hereafter by our own actions, we will hardly even notice a mortal lifetime in prison."

"A neat theory. What are you in for?" Tallon asked out of politeness, but all he really wanted to do was to sit in the sun and doze. He had discovered he could still dream, and in dreams his brown plastic eyes were as good as real eyes.

"I'm a doctor of medicine. I came here from Louisiana when this planet was first reached. It wasn't called Emm Luther in those days, of course. I put a lifetime of hard work into this world, and I love it. So when it broke away from the empire I worked to bring it back to its true destiny."

Tallon snorted with bitter amusement. "I take it that when you get down to the practical details of working to bring a world back to its true destiny, the job includes getting rid of obstinate politicians?"

"Well, son, we had a saying back home that you can't reason a man out of something he hasn't been reasoned into. So . . ."

"So you're in prison doing life for something that would have got you the same sentence, or worse, under any other political regime." Tallon spoke angrily, and there was a long silence when he had finished. An insect hummed near his face, then drifted away in the warm air.

"I'm surprised to hear you speak like that, son. I thought we'd have common interests, but I fear I've intruded. I'll go."

Tallon nodded and listened as Winfield struggled heavily to his feet. Again something flicked lightly against his leg. This time he grabbed for it and found himself holding the end of a cane.

"My apologies," Winfield said. "The cane is an ancient device for the members of our fraternity, but it is undeniably useful. Without it I would have fallen over your legs, with consequent embarrassment to both parties."

A few seconds passed before Tallon absorbed the full meaning of the other man's rounded, rolling phrases.

"Hold on a minute. Do you mean that you're——?"

"*Blind* is the word, son. You get used to saying it after a few years."

"Why didn't you tell me earlier? I didn't know. Please sit down again." Tallon's hand found the man's arm and held on. Winfield seemed to consider the idea; then he sat down, again with furious grunting. Tallon guessed he was very fat and out of condition. He found Winfield's pomposity irritating, especially his use of the word son, but here was a man who had already explored the road Tallon was destined to walk. They sat in silence for a while, listening to the rhythmic crunch of gravel as the rest of the prisoners exercised in another part of the yard.

"I expect you're wondering if I lost my sight in the same manner as you," Winfield finally said.

"Well, yes."

"No, son. Nothing quite so dramatic. Eight years ago I tried to escape from this place with the idea of working my way back to Earth. I got as far as the swamp. That's the easy part, of course; anybody can reach the swamp. It's getting to the other side that counts. There's a rather nasty species of chigger out there. The gravid females go for your eyes. When the guards brought me back to the Pavilion I was well on the way to having a nest of the brutes breeding in each eye.

"Dr. Heck had quite a job to keep them from going through to the brain. He was deliriously happy for nearly a week—whistled Gilbert and Sullivan the whole time."

Tallon was appalled. "But what were you hoping to do supposing you had managed to get through the swamp? The space terminal at New Wittenburg is a thousand miles from here, and even if it were only a thousand yards away, you could never have passed through the checkpoints."

"Son," Winfield sounded sad, "your mind is too preoccupied with details. I admire a man who has an eye for detail, but not if he lets it negate his attitude to the master plan."

"*Plan!* What plan? All you had was a crazy notion you could get up and walk a few light-centuries back to Louisiana."

"Progress is the history of crazy notions, Sam. Su-

28

praluctic flight itself was a crazy notion till somebody made it work. I can't believe you are prepared to rot in this place for the rest of your life."

"I may not be prepared for it, but I'm going to do it."

"Even if I offered to take you with me next time?" Winfield's voice had sunk to a whisper.

Tallon laughed aloud for the first time since the morning McNulty had limped into his office and handed him a piece of paper containing the cosmic address of a new planet. "Go away, old man," he said. "You really had me going for a minute. Now I want to rest my ears."

Winfield kept talking. "It's going to be entirely different next time. I was unprepared for the swamp before, but I've been getting ready for it for eight years. I assure you, I *know* how to get through."

"But you're blind! You'd have trouble crossing a children's playground."

"Blind," Winfield said mysteriously, "but not blind."

"Talking," Tallon replied in similar tones, "but not talking sense."

"Listen to this, son." Winfield moved closer until his breath was brushing Tallon's ear. He smelled of bread and butter. "You've had training in electronics. You know that back on Earth, and on most other worlds, too, a blind person can get many kinds of aids."

"That's a different case, isn't it, Doc? Emm Luther's electronics industry is part and parcel of its space-probe program. Every electronics specialist on the planet works on the program or on associated priority projects, or else is away on this new planet they've found. Besides, the Temporal Moderator has ruled that it's against the creed to join man-made parts to bodies fashioned in the Divine Image. The gadgets you're talking about simply don't exist in this part of the galaxy."

"But they do," Winfield said triumphantly. "Or they almost do. I'm building a primitive sonar torch in the prison rehabilitation center. At least, Ed Hogarth, who runs the center's workshop, is building it under my direction. I can't do the actual work myself, naturally."

Tallon sighed resignedly. It looked as though Winfield's conversation was made up of absurd statements and fantasy.

"You mean they don't watch you in there? Don't they mind that two of the government's strictest injunctions are being broken with government equipment in a government establishment?"

Winfield rose noisily to his feet. "Son, you have an

29

unfortunate skeptical attitude, but I'm going to assume that in less trying circumstances you are capable of civilized behavior. Come with me."

"Where?"

"To the workshop. You have one or two surprises in store."

Holding on to Winfield's plump arm, Tallon followed him from the quadrangle, aware that his curiosity was aroused as he had never expected it to be again. Winfield moved confidently and quite quickly, tapping with his cane. As they walked a succession of men touched Tallon's arm in sympathetic greeting, and one pushed a pack of cigarettes into his free hand. He struggled to keep his head up and walk boldly, but it was almost impossible, and he could feel the fixed apologetic smile of a sightless man engraving itself on his face.

To reach the workshop of the rehabilitation center they had to pass the main prison building and walk two hundred yards to an auxiliary block. During the walk Winfield explained that his torch generated a narrow beam of inaudible high-frequency sound and had a receiver to pick up the echoes; an electronic device combined the outgoing and returning sounds. The idea was that the sound generator would sweep repeatedly from about 80 to 40 kilocycles a second, so that at any instant the outgoing signal would be at a slightly lower frequency than any of the echoes. Combining the two would produce a beat frequency proportional to the distance of any object in the torch's beam and thus allow a blind man to build up a picture of his surroundings.

Winfield had partly worked out the theory, and partly remembered it from articles in old technomedical journals. Ed Hogarth, who apparently was a compulsive gadgeteer, had built him a prototype, but was having trouble with the electronics of the frequency-reduction stage, which should have rendered the high-pitched beats audible to the human ear.

As he listened, Tallon felt a growing respect for the old doctor, who seemed genuinely incapable of accepting defeat. They reached the rehabilitation center and stopped at the entrance.

"Just one thing before we go in, son. I want you to promise not to say anything to Ed about the real reason why I want the torch built. If he guessed, he would quit work on it immediately—to save me from myself, as the saying goes."

Tallon said, "All right, but I want you to make me one promise in return. If you really do have an escape plan, don't include me in it. If I ever decide to commit suicide I'll pick an easier way."

They went up a flight of stairs and into the workshop. Tallon identified it at once by the familiar smell of hot solder and stale cigarette smoke, a smell that had not changed since his student days.

"Are you there, Ed?" The echoes from Winfield's voice suggested the workshop was quite small. "I've brought a visitor."

"I *know* you've brought a visitor," a thin, irritable voice said from close by. "I can see him, can't I? You've been blind so long you've begun to think nobody else can see." The voice faded into barely audible swearing.

Winfield gave his booming laugh and whispered to Tallon, "Ed was born on this planet, but he was very active in the old Unionist movement at one time and didn't have enough sense to quit when the Lutherians took over. He was arrested by Kreuger and suffered an unfortunate accident to his heels while trying to get free. There are quite a few of Kreuger's prizes hopping about the Pavilion like birds."

"And my ears are all right, too," Hogarth's voice warned.

"Ed, this is Sam Tallon—the man who almost finished Cherkassky. He's an electronics expert, so perhaps you'll get my torch working now."

"I have a degree in electronics," Tallon said. "That isn't the same as being an expert."

"But you'll be able to get the bugs out of a simple frequency-reducer circuit," Winfield said. "Here, feel this."

He drew Tallon over to a bench and placed his hands on a complicated metal and plastic object about three feet square.

"Is that it?" Tallon explored the massive circuitry with his fingers. "What good is this thing to you? I thought you were talking about something you could carry in one hand."

"It's a model," Hogarth snapped impatiently, "twenty times the size of the real instrument. That lets the doctor feel out what he thinks he's doing, and I reproduce it in proper size. It's a good idea, except it doesn't work."

"It'll work now," Winfield said confidently. "What do you say, son?"

Tallon thought it over. Winfield seemed to be a crazy old coot, and in all probability Hogarth was another, but in the brief time he had spent with them, he had almost forgotten about being blind. "I'll help," he said. "Have you materials to build two prototypes?"

Winfield squeezed his hand excitedly. "Don't worry about that part, son. Helen will see we get all the parts we need."

"Helen?"

"Yes. Helen Juste. She's head of the rehabilitation center."

"And she doesn't object to your building this thing?"

"Object!" Winfield roared. "It was mainly her idea. She's been behind the scheme from the start."

Tallon shook his head in disbelief. "Isn't that a strange thing for a senior government officer to do? Why should she risk appearing before the doctrinal synod just to help you?"

"There you go again, son—letting your concern for petty detail hinder the grand scheme. How should I know why she does it? Perhaps she likes my eyes; Dr. Heck tells me they're a rather pretty shade of blue. Of course he's prejudiced, since he made them himself."

Both Winfield and Hogarth laughed extravagantly. Tallon put his hands on the blocky shape of the frequency-reducer model, where he could feel sunlight warming his skin. All his preconceived notions had been wrong. The life of a blind man was proving to be neither dull nor simple.

six

Tallon positioned the sonar torch carefully on his forehead, slipped the earpiece into his right ear, and switched on. He stood up, moved his head about experimentally, and began to walk. He was suddenly aware of how much he had gotten used to feeling his way with a cane.

The range of the torch was set for five yards, which meant anything beyond that distance would produce no echo. As he advanced he moved his head first horizontally, then vertically. The latter movement produced a tone that could be compared to an inverted vee as the sonar beam, now touching the ground, approached his feet and receded again.

Tallon forced himself to walk smoothly and steadily, giving all his attention to the rising and falling electronic tone. He had covered about ten yards when he began to pick up a tiny *blip* near the top of each vertical scan. Still walking, but more slowly now, he concentrated on the upper part of the sweep. The *blip* crept higher up the tonal scale with each appearance, and finally Tallon was able to convert it into a shrill steady note by inclining his head slightly downward.

He put his hand out and touched a metal bar suspended just below eye level.

"Wonderful! That's really wonderful!" The woman's voice sounded young and fresh, and it took him by surprise. He turned toward it self-consciously, wondering how he looked in sloppy prison clothing, with a plastic box strapped to his forehead, then was surprised at his reaction. Apparently his male ego still considered itself in the running, undaunted by plastic buttons in place of eyes. In the sonar he picked up the slightly discordant tone produced by a human being.

"Miss Juste?"

"Yes. Dr. Winfield and Ed told me you were making excellent progress with the sonar, but I didn't realize you had got so far with it. I'm glad I came to see for myself."

"The work passes the time," Tallon smiled uncertainly.

He felt strangely uneasy, as though he had almost remembered something important, then let it slip away. Perhaps this would be as good a time as any to start probing her motives.

"It's very good of you to let us do this sort of thing in view of the . . . climate of official opinion."

There was silence for a few seconds, then Tallon heard the familiar sound of Winfield's cane and Hogarth's crutches approaching across the concrete apron they were using for the sonar trials.

"Well, Miss Juste," Winfield said, "what did you think of that?"

"I'm very impressed. I was just saying so to Detainee Tallon. Is any more work needed on an instrument that operates so well?"

Tallon noticed her use of the word Detainee in his case, in contrast to her informal way of referring to Winfield and Hogarth. He kept the sonar beam on her, silently cursing its shortcomings. As far as the beam was concerned, there was no significant difference between a crane driver and a showgirl. He felt the first stirrings of an idea.

"The preliminary tests are just about completed," Winfield announced proudly. "Sam and I will be wearing the sonars permanently from now on to gain experience with them. It will take a few weeks to sort out the best range selection and settle on the optimum beam width."

"I see. Well, let me know how you get on."

"Of course, Miss Juste. Thank you for all your kindness."

Tallon heard her firm light steps move away; then he turned to Winfield. Distinguishing between Winfield and Hogarth with the beam was easy, because the doctor stood head and shoulders above his crippled companion. To demonstrate his increasing mastery over the sonar, Tallon touched Winfield accurately on the shoulder.

"You know, Logan, you could be making a mistake in not providing in your grand scheme for an analysis of Miss Juste's motivation. She doesn't strike me as the sort of girl who does things without a reason."

"There he goes," Hogarth grumbled. "Knows more about Miss Juste than we do, and he's never even seen her. This boy must have been a mean card player when he had eyes."

Tallon grinned. At first he had been disconcerted by the Hogarth's constant and uninhibited references to his blindness; then he had realized that they were good for his

34

sense of proportion and were uttered for that very reason.

In the afternoon Tallon and Winfield went for a walk using their sonars for guidance. They confined themselves to circuits of an unused tennis court, which was out of bounds to all but disabled prisoners. No guards questioned them about the boxes strapped to their foreheads, and Tallon guessed Helen Juste had given instructions for them to be left alone. He had noticed, too, that none of the medical staff had spoken to them about the sonar project. He asked Winfield how much influence the woman had in the administration of the Pavilion.

"I'm not sure," Winfield replied. "I've heard she's related to the Moderator himself. I've been told that the rehabilitation center was her own idea, and that the Moderator pulled strings to get it set up. Occupational therapy isn't good doctrine, you know. The synod recommends prayer and fasting for intransigents such as us."

"But would the Moderator stretch the rules that far?"

"Son, you take everything too literally. A few years in practical politics would have done you a world of good. Listen, if the head of a government orders his people to cut down on liquor because their drunkenness is ruining the country's economy, it doesn't mean he's going to drink less himself. Nor would he expect his relatives and friends to change their drinking habits. That's human nature."

"You make it all sound so simple," Tallon said impatiently. He decided to broach the idea that had come to him during his talk with Helen Juste. "Are you still working on your grand plan to break out of the Pavilion?"

"Son, if I can't die on Earth, I may not die at all. Are you coming with me?"

"I've told you how I feel about that, but maybe I can help you."

"How?"

"Do you think Miss Juste would get us a couple of television cameras? The peanut-size jobs used for bugging people's apartments? They probably have them all over the prison."

Winfield stopped walking and sank his fingers into Tallon's arm. "Do you mean what I think you mean?"

"Yes, why not? We both have our optic nerves intact. It's only a matter of converting the camera output to the right sort of signal and feeding it into the nerve endings. It's a common technique on Earth."

"But wouldn't it involve surgery? I doubt if——"

"No surgery needed if we beam the signal accurately through the eye. The fact that we have plastic skins on

35

our eyes could help, because we could insert a simple X and Y plate arrangement in the plastic to keep the beam aimed at the nerve ending, regardless of eye movements."

Winfield began to tremble with excitement. "If I could see again, and with the preparations I've made for the swamp, I'd be walking down the main street in Natchitoches inside a year. I *know* it." His normally powerful voice sounded strangely small.

"Well, that's the grand plan," Tallon said. "Now we have to consider some of those petty details of mine. We'll need the cameras and a range of microminiature components. And we'll have to have access to the appropriate journals and an auto-reader—you'll absorb the physiological data; I'll do the semiconductor research."

"But who will build the units? Ed knows nothing about that sort of work."

"That's another detail. You'll have to ask Miss Juste for the use of an assembly robot—Grade 2 at least— programmed for microminiature electronics. They probably have one in their maintenance lab."

"But, my God, Sam! Those things cost over half a million."

"Ask her anyway. She'll arrange it for you. Remember, she likes the color of your eyes."

Tallon stood for a moment, face turned toward the hot white sun of Emm Luther, experiencing a rare moment of certitude.

A week later two guards dragged the assembly robot into the center's workshop on a negative-gravity sled.

Tallon had spent most of the week practicing with his sonar and, between times, trying to understand what had happened to him the first day he had spoken to Helen Juste. A psychic explosion, a violent upheaval in his subconscious—and for no reason at all. He ruled out all the vaguely para-normal phenomena sometimes associated with romantic love, partly out of natural skepticism, partly because he had never even seen her. Hogarth had described her as a spindly redhead with orange eyes, so she did not seem the sort of woman who might have a deeply disturbing effect on him or on any other man. And even had she been a raven-haired myth-woman, there was no real explanation for the abrupt shift in his perception by which he had *known* she would let them have the equipment. As he lay in his cell each night, awaiting the pale light of dreams, he returned to the problem again and again, trying to wrest some significance from it.

But once the robot was installed and the work of

36

writing its program begun, Tallon found himself with nothing on his mind but the project. Winfield and he spent weeks in which every waking hour, apart from mealtimes and the compulsory prayer sessions, was spent in the prison library, listening to auto-readers. Most of the available journals were out of date, because their importation from Earth had never been encouraged by the Lutheran government and, in recent years, had been practically banned by Earth. The latter move was a sign of the deterioration in relations between the two since the brand-new planet of Aitch Mühlenberg had dropped into Emm Luther's lap; but the information was there just the same.

As he worked on it Tallon felt his mind sink through the layers the years had superimposed on his personality. A younger Sam Tallon emerged, one who had been determined to carve out a career in domain physics, until some unremembered event had diverted him into world-hopping, and then finally to the Block and all it represented. The contentment Tallon experienced was so profound, he began to suspect that a subconscious drive toward it had been his real motivation for initiating the artificial-eye project—not the desire to regain his own sight or help Winfield, but a powerful need to re-create himself as he was ... *when?* And why should a single encounter with Helen Juste have triggered the impulse? He had no memories of any girl with red hair and unusual eyes who might have been a proto-Helen.

As the computer program took shape they put the assembly robot to work on two identical prototypes of what, for lack of inspiration, they named eyesets. Supplementing the program, with its own vast store of instructions built into it for microminiature electronics, the robot slowly assembled two pairs of spectacles in the vacuum-locked privacy of its sterile belly. They were conventional in appearance, except for the beads that were the television cameras mounted on the bridge pieces. The rims served to direct the microwaves back into the eyes.

The only problem Tallon and Winfield had to handle themselves—through Ed Hogarth's hands—was that of keeping the beams focused accurately on the optic nerve. They solved it by an adaption of Tallon's original plan—a single metal plug at the edge of each plastic iris. The theory was that every eye movement would bring the metal plug to a new position in a weak magnetic field generated inside the spectacle frame, thus providing reference data for a single-crystal computer, which redirected the beams accordingly.

37

By the time he had reached the final part of the program, which dealt with the circuitry for the infinitely more subtle language of the glial cells, Tallon was wholly committed to the intellectual adventure. He scarcely touched his meals and was losing weight steadily.

The month-long reverie came to an end one afternoon as he lay in the sound-cone of an auto-reader.

He recognized Winfield's approach by the quick, nervous tapping of the cane, which the old man still used in conjunction with the sonar torch.

"I've got to speak to you right away, son. Sorry to interrupt, but it's important." Winfield's voice was hoarse with urgency.

"It's all right, Doc. What's the trouble?" Tallon swung his legs from the couch and rolled out of the sound area.

"The trouble is Cherkassky. The grapevine says he's out of the hospital."

"What of it? He can't touch me in here."

"That's the point, son. They say he still isn't fit for normal duty, but he has arranged to join the Pavilion staff for a 'working convalescence.' You know what that means, don't you? You know why he's coming here?"

Of their own accord, Tallon's hands rose to his face, and the finger tips gently traced the curve of his unseeing, plastic eyes. "Yes, Doc," he said quietly. "Thanks for telling me. I know why he's coming here."

seven

Light—fierce and steady.
Pain—fierce and steady!

Tallon snatched off the eyeset and sat contracted in the chair, waiting for the needling agony to subside. He knew his eyes would have been streaming with tears had the glands not been ripped away by the darts of Cherkassky's hornet gun. The pain took a long time to recede, occasionally reaching its former level again, like a reluctant ebb tide.

"What's the matter, Sam—no better?" Hogarth sounded cool and disinterested, which meant he was alarmed.

Tallon shook his head. "We're not getting it. Something is seriously wrong with the conversion stage. The signals the nerve expects and the signals we're feeding into it just aren't compatible—and they hurt so much I can't even look for tuning responses.

"We took on a big job, son," Winfield said sadly. "Perhaps too big, under the circumstances."

"That's not it. We were going well, right up to the last stage. The synthesis of the glial code was the only really tough part, but it was coming all right. I was *drinking* it, till I heard about our friend Cherkassky."

"It was only a rumor. The grapevine has been wrong before."

"Perhaps, but the effect's the same whether the rumor's true or false. I can't hold the concept now. I just can't say for certain if we've built in a basic error or merely have to chase out a few bugs. How about a local anaesthetic to kill the pain while I examine what we're getting?"

"No good. You could crisp your optic nerves."

"Then what in hell do we do? We've already wasted two weeks trying to synthesize something that every moronic beast that ever walked or flew or swam can do without even trying. It isn't right that—Christ!" Tallon shouted with excitement as a new kind of light seared through his mind.

39

"Take it easy," Winfield warned uneasily. "You know the penalities for blasphemy on this planet."

"I wasn't blaspheming. Doc, I know where we can pick up the whole visual-electrical complex. The lot—rod-and-cone, bipolars, ganglions, glials—the whole process absolutely ready-made. Ready for us to lift off the rack and put it on."

"Where?"

"Right here in the workshop. Ed's eyes are all right, aren't they?"

Hogarth whinnied with alarm. "My eyes are fine, and I aim to keep them that way, you damned Earthside ghoul. Leave my eyes out of it."

"We will, but your eyes won't leave us alone. They're bombarding us and everything around you with exactly the information the doctor and I need. Every kink in your optic nerves is spraying us with electrons. You're a little radio station, Ed, and your tape jockey plays only one tune—the glial code."

"My mother was right," Hogarth said reflectively. "She always knew I would make good."

"You sound excited, Sam." Winfield's voice was sober. "Do you think you're getting it this time?"

"This time I've got it."

Four days later, as dawn was beginning to overpaint the fainter stars, Tallon saw Winfield for the first time.

He sat perfectly still for a moment, savoring the miracle of vision, feeling humbled by the sudden stark revelation of the pinnacle of human technology upon which his triumph was poised: the centuries of research into the complex language of glial-cell transients; the development of assembly robots and micro-Waldos; the growth of cybernetic philosophies that enabled a man to incorporate a billion electronic circuits in a single chip of crystal and use only those that served his purpose, without his ever knowing which circuits they were.

"Tell us the worst, son."

"It's all right, Doc; it works. I can see you. The trouble is I can see myself as well."

Tallon gave a sharp laugh and fought to adjust to the supremely unnatural situation of having a body in one place and eyes in another. For the first trial of the new eyeset, he and Winfield sat close together at one end of the workshop while Hogarth remained at the other end with strict instructions not to take his gaze off them. Tallon had not moved, but his new eyes told him he was

40

at the other side of the room, looking at both Winfield and *himself*.

The doctor was remarkably like the mental picture Tallon had formed of him—a red-faced, silver-haired old giant. He held a cane in one hand, and his head, to which was strapped the gray box of his sonar torch, was in the upright, alert attitude of a blind man.

Tallon examined himself curiously. His face behind the eyeset frame looked longer and more thoughtful than ever, and the loose brown Pavilion overalls showed that he had lost about fifteen pounds since coming to the prison. Otherwise he looked much as he always had, something Tallon found surprising, considering how he felt. His attention came back to Winfield, whose face was taut with concentration as he waited to hear what Tallon would have to say.

"Relax, Doc. I told you—it works perfectly. I'm just getting used to seeing myself as others see me."

Winfield smiled; then Tallon gasped and grabbed the sides of his chair for support as the workshop seemed to swing away from beneath his feet, right itself, and go bounding past him.

"Hold it, Ed!" he shouted frantically. "Don't jump about like that. Remember you've got me with you."

"I don't care," Hogarth said. "I'm going to shake your hand. I had my doubts about you, Sam, but you're a bright boy in spite of your college education."

"Thanks, Ed." Tallon watched in fascination as his own image grew larger and closer and Ed's busily working metal crutches flickered on the lower edge of Tallon's field of vision. He held out his hand and noticed that *other* Sam Tallon perform an identical movement. Finally he saw Hogarth's thin hand come into view and grasp his. The touch of fingers, coming at precisely the right moment indicated by the actions of the tableau of strangers, was like an electric shock.

Tallon took the eyeset off with his free hand, plunging himself into friendly darkness, and struggled not to be sick. For a moment the disorientation had been complete.

"Your turn now," he said, holding the eyeset out to Winfield. "Pull them off as soon as you get into trouble, and don't be too alarmed at how you feel."

"Thanks, son. I'll feel just fine."

Feeling slightly uncomfortable, Tallon sat while the doctor tried out the eyeset. The old man had been blind for eight years and was likely to experience an even bigger shock than had Tallon. As far as quality of vision was concerned, the eyeset worked perfectly, but perhaps he had not given enough consideration to the implications of seeing only—and precisely—what could be seen by the one whose nerve impulses he was pirating. From a practical point of view, a poorer quality image picked up by a receptor located right on the eyeset would be much better. On the other hand, if he had something like a trained squirrel to sit on his shoulder . . .

"For God's sake, Ed," Winfield boomed, "hold that bony little head of yours in one place for a few seconds. You're making me seasick."

"What's going on here?" Hogarth sounded indignant. "Whose head is it, anyway? Nobody thanks me for the use of my eyes; they only act as if they've taken over my head."

"Don't worry, Ed," Tallon reassured him. "You can have it back when we've finished with it."

Hogarth sniffed and lapsed into his customary semi-audible swearing. Winfield again demonstrated his characteristic stubbornness by keeping the eyeset on longer than Tallon had, and ordering Hogarth to go to the windows and look in directions that he called out to him. Tallon listened in awe as the old man gave noisy sighs of appreciation or furious commands of "eyes right" or "eyes left," while Hogarth's swearing grew louder and more violent. It all came to an end suddenly.

"The eyeset has stopped working," Winfield announced. "It's broken."

"It isn't," Hogarth said triumphantly. "I've got my hands over my eyes."

"You treacherous little weasel," Winfield said in a thunderstruck whisper, then began to laugh. Tallon and Hogarth joined in, spilling the tension that had been building up in them for weeks.

When they finally stopped laughing Tallon discovered he was both hungry and exhausted. He got the eyeset back and watched as Hogarth put the other prototype, still unmodified, onto the work platform of the assembly robot. He saw the little man's hands flick out, as though from Tallon's own body, and press the starter buttons. The robot's doors slid across, enclosing the eyeset, and there was a hiss as the air was expelled from its interior. For the sort of work it was going to do, even the molecules of the atmosphere had to be excluded.

Tallon stood up and patted his stomach. "Isn't it about time for breakfast?"

Hogarth remained seated at the robot's control console.

"It is, but I think I'll stay on here till this gadget's finished. Some of the boys are getting a bit sore about the way I've been keeping them out lately. I don't want them coming in and upsetting things at this stage."

"I'll stay on too, son. That's *my* eyeset in there, and I don't mind waiting a few hours to get my hands on it. If you're agreeable, I'll send word to Miss Juste and let her know we can give her a demonstration this afternoon."

Tallon found the thought of actually seeing Helen Juste strangely alarming. She had not been back at the center's workshop since the day she saw the sonar torch in operation, and the inexplicable turmoil the meeting had created within him was beginning to die down. He had no wish to churn it up again, and yet . . .

"Sure. That's all right with me, Doc. Well, I'm going to catch up on some of the food I've been missing out on. Sorry to bother you again, Ed, but would you mind watching me till I get out through the door?"

Tallon decided to rely entirely on the eyeset. He left his sonar and cane on the bench, then walked to the door. As he moved he concentrated on the image of his own receding back, as seen by Hogarth, and was able to guide his hand accurately to the door handle. He took a deep breath and opened the door.

"You're on your own now, son," Winfield called after him.

Tallon was still able to pick up vision from Hogarth when he was on the upper landing, but now it was a handicap. He slid the control on the right-hand arm of the eyeset frame to "passive" and went down the stairs in darkness. Once through the outer door he moved the control to "search and hold," and selected maximum range. Men were moving toward the mess hall in twos and threes, and almost immediately Tallon was looking through the eyes of another prisoner.

The man must have been walking with his head down, for Tallon saw nothing but feet striding across the white concrete. Keeping the control at "search and hold," he flicked the first "reject" stud. He had included six of these studs in the design so that the eyeset would temporarily memorize up to six individual signal patterns and let him reselect any of them at will. A seventh stud was provided to clear the little memory unit.

Tallon had more luck this time. He was looking through the eyes of a tall man who was moving easily, with head erect, toward a low building—presumably the mess hall—at the edge of a large plaza. Other blocks of two and three storys lined the square, and Tallon had no idea which of them was the center's workshop. He put his arms up and waved, as though to a friend, and saw himself—a tiny figure standing at the entrance of the second building to the right of the mess hall.

Tallon waited until his host had neared the workshop; then he walked quickly out from the entrance toward him, narrowly missing a strolling guard, and fell in about three paces in front. Once or twice through force of habit, he tried to look back over his shoulder, but saw only his own face, white and slightly desperate, turning briefly toward his host.

At the entrance to the mess hall a certain amount of jostling was going on where the groups converged, and the host caught up with him. Tallon found himself staring at the back of his own head from a distance of a few inches. Although disconcerting, the very proximity made it easier for Tallon to steer himself through the inner door and to an empty seat at one of the long tables. His host went farther up the hall and sat down, facing in a direction that excluded Tallon from the man's field of vision. Fingering the eyeset frame, Tallon cleared the memory unit, switched to the minimum range of six feet, and let the "search and hold" start over again. There was a momentary haze of light as the eyeset picked up several signals at once before singling out one of them. Again he was lucky: This time he was looking through the eyes of the man at the opposite side of the table.

By the time the turret-shaped serving robot moved along the table's central slot to dispense breakfasts, Tallon's stomach was knotted with tension. He ate the full meal, however; he felt he had earned it.

Tallon and Winfield, both wearing eyesets, stood at attention as Helen Juste walked into the workshop. Hogarth, being crippled, was not obliged to do anything more than look respectful, but he raised himself as high as his crutches would allow.

Helen Juste smiled at Hogarth and motioned to him to sit down. Tallon, who was tuned in on Hogarth, also received the smile, and he responded instinctively before remembering it had not been directed at him. He saw what Hogarth meant when he'd described her as a spindly redhead with orange eyes, and at the same time he marveled at how any man could have dismissed the phenomenon of Helen Juste with such a phrase. She was slim, not spindly, and everything was in proportion, giving her sleekly economical lines that would have thrilled a star-class designer of humanoid robots. Her hair was a rich coppery brown, and her eyes were the color—Tallon sought an exact comparison—of aged whiskey in fire-lit crystal. He found himself whispering one word over and over again—yes, yes, yes. . . .

She stayed for almost an hour, showing intense interest in the eyesets, questioning Winfield closely about their operation and performance. The doctor protested several times that his was not the brain behind the eyesets, but although she glanced at Tallon on those occasions, she did not speak to him. Tallon found himself rather pleased at this, satisfied at having been placed in a special category.

As she was leaving she asked Winfield if they were finished with the assembly robot.

"I'm not sure," Winfield said. "I expect the maintenance shop staff want it back in a hurry, but we've done almost no field work with the eyesets. There might be minor modifications needed; in fact, Detainee Tallon is not really satisfied with the basic concept. I think he wants to try again with a camera-based system."

Helen Juste looked doubtful. "Well, as you know, I've been trying to introduce to the prison board the idea that they might have special responsibilities to those detainees who have suffered disablement. But there's a limit to how much I can do in this direction." She hesitated. "I'm going on leave in three days; the equipment must be returned by then."

Winfield gave a military-style salute. "We sincerely thank you, Miss Juste."

She went out, and Tallon thought her eyes flickered once, speculatively, in his direction, but Hogarth's gaze was already turning away so Tallon could not be sure. He was depressed by her reminder that there was a world outside the Pavilion, and that she still belonged to it.

"I thought she was going to stay all day," Hogarth complained bitterly, lighting his pipe. "I can't stand that skinny dame coming into my shop."

Tallon snorted. "You still have your eyes, Ed, but you don't know how to use them."

"Well spoken, son," Winfield boomed. "Did you notice he hardly looked at her legs once? The first time in eight years I get a chance to look at a woman, and the old goat in charge of the eyes keeps staring out the window!"

Tallon smiled, but he noticed he was seeing nothing but a close-up of Hogarth's pipe, with one gnarled finger pressing the gray ash down into the blackened bowl. He got an impression the little man was worried. "What is it, Ed?"

"Did either of you lady-killers go to the recreation block today to hear the newscast?"

"No."

"Well, you should've. The negotiations between Emm Luther and Earth over the new planet have broken down. The Earthside delegates finally realized the Moderator is prepared to stall forever, and they walked out of the conference. It looks like we'll soon be in the middle of the first interstellar war the empire has ever seen."

Tallon put one hand on his temple; he had been forcing himself to forget all about the Block and the bead-sized capsule that nourished a fragment of his own brain. The thought that the little sphere of gray tissue could be equated with the green-blue immensity of a fertile world was insupportable. "That's bad," he said quietly.

"There's more. The grapevine has it definite about Cherkassky. He's coming here next week."

Tallon continued to speak calmly in spite of the sudden hammering in his chest. "Doc, we haven't really tested our new eyes yet. I think we ought to try a long walk."

"You mean a really long walk?"

Tallon nodded soberly. It was a thousand miles to New Wittenburg and eighty thousand portals back to Earth.

eight

Cronin, the bird man, looked up at them with growing suspicion in his red-rimmed eyes. "No," he said. "I've no owls, or hawks, or any birds like that. I tell you, we don't have enough small vermin this far south to attract them. Why do you have to have a hunting bird?"

"We don't," Tallon replied quickly. "We'll take two of those brown ones that look like doves. Just so long as they're tame enough to stay with us and not fly off."

He had wanted predatory birds because their eye positions corresponded roughly to a human's, which meant it would be easier to get used to their form of vision. It would be good to have a vision center close to his own body, but Tallon was not happy about the idea of apparently seeing out of each side of his head. The main thing, however, was to get hold of some usable optical system in a hurry.

"Well, I don't know about all this." The bird man looked sharply at Tallon. "Say, aren't you Tallon? I thought you were blind or something."

"I am—almost. That's why I want the birds. They'd be a bit like guide dogs."

"Mmmm, I don't know. You guys don't look like bird-lovers to me. Birds are sensitive, you know."

Winfield coughed impatiently. "We'll give you four cartons of cigarettes for each. I understand that's twice the standard rate."

Detainee Cronin shrugged and lifted two of the dovelike native birds from the little wire-mesh aviary he had built on the southern end of the peninsula. He tied short lengths of cord to the legs of the docile, quivering birds and handed them over.

"If you want them to sit on your shoulders, tie them to your epaulettes for a couple of days till they get used to you."

Tallon thanked him, and they hurried away with the birds. Near the crumbling walls of the original Pavilion gardens they stopped and transferred the birds to their shoulders. When Tallon selected his bird's visual signals on a proximity basis, he felt as though the top had been lifted from his head, letting the light pour in. The bird's widely spaced eyes provided Tallon with a brilliant 360-degree view of land, sea, and sky. This vision, which enabled the bird to spot hunters and other enemies, gave Tallon a feeling of being hunted. It was difficult to get used to having his own ear looming up on one side of his field of vision, but there was the consolation that nobody could take him by surprise.

They walked to the eastern side of the peninsula, where the ground rose to a low cliff, giving them a view out across the tideless, planet-spanning ocean. Tallon was entranced by the sensation of airy spaciousness and freedom. He felt that—if he could only remember how—he could take a deep breath and soar upward over the sunlit curve of the world.

Winfield pointed northward. Beyond the Pavilion's crenelated rooftops, shimmering in the afternoon light, was a wall of mist. Clustered at its base were blooms, brilliant red beacons that were visible from more than a mile away.

"That's the swamp. There's about four miles of it before you reach the mainland proper."

"Wouldn't it be easier to swim along one side?"

"You'd have to swim out to sea for a mile or more to get round the stuff that grows out from the swamp; and the air patrols would spot you right off. No—the only way is straight up the center. There's one big advantage about going through the swamp: We'll be presumed dead within a few hours, and they won't search very hard on the far side. In fact, I think all they'll do is make a daily check on the magazines of the rattler rifles to see if there's any record of us having been picked off."

"Rattler rifles?"

"Yes. Did I forget to mention them?" Winfield chuckled mirthlessly.

The northern edge of the swamp was an irregular line extending six miles across the peninsula. The improbability of any prisoner ever reaching it had persuaded the Pavilion's security consultants to forego the trouble and expense of manned patrols along the boundary. Instead, a chain of forty pylons, equipped with robot rifles, had been erected. Each rifle had two widely spaced heat-sensitive cups, like those on a rattlesnake's head, which enabled it to train itself and fire at any warm-blooded being coming into range. They fired heat-seeking missiles, an inch in diameter, equipped with tiny pulse motors that gave them a constant velocity of seven thousand feet a second. The rifles had rarely gone into action against humans, but their effectiveness had been demonstrated in other ways. Within a week of their installation every warm-blooded animal indigenous to the swamp had been blasted into crimson ooze and bone fragments.

"If the rifles are that good," Tallon said, "how do we get by them? How do we even get near them?"

"Come along and I'll show you."

They crossed the peninsula south of the Pavilion and walked along the western shore until the prison buildings were behind them and the ice-green mists of the swamp swirled into the sky close ahead. A simple log palisade, topped with barbed wire, marked the limits of the Pavilion grounds; beyond it, the sculptured convolutions of the swamp mist hung motionless in the air. Tallon had not been that close before and had not realized how utterly inimical the swamp really was. Stray currents of air brought him wisps of its breath—clammy cold, and heavy with a stink that caused an unpleasant surge in his belly.

"Rich, isn't it? We aren't likely to overeat in there," Winfield said, with an almost proprietary pride. "Now don't point or do anything suspicious, in case they're watching us from the tower, but have a look at the palisade close to that white rock. Do you see where I mean?"

Tallon nodded.

"That part is hollow, full of a kind of wood-boring worm. The maintenance team goes right round the palisade twice a year, spraying it with a penetrant insecticide to keep the worms down. I come along first and paint that area with ordinary wood sealer to keep the insecticide out. There are a couple of million worms in there who must think of me as God.

"Nice work; but wouldn't it have been easier to go over the top?"

"For you, yes. I'm not built for climbing. Eight years ago I made it and no more, and my shadow has increased considerably since then."

"You were going to tell me about the rifles."

"Yes. See those creepers with the deep red flowers, right at the edge of the swamp? Those are *dringo* plants. The leaves are over a quarter of an inch thick, and they're tough enough to take sewing together. We'll bring needles and thread and make screens to get us past the rifles."

49

"You're sure they're good insulators?" Tallon asked doubtfully.

"They have to be. A species of leaping scorpion that can't stand temperature variations lives under those leaves. They get pretty mad when you pluck their cover away. But don't worry; we'll be protected."

"That's the other thing I was going to ask you about."

"It's all in the plan, son. Close to that same white rock there's a small fissure in the ground. It was one of the places I could find without any trouble, even when I couldn't see. That's where the escape kits are hidden."

"Kits plural?"

"Yes. I was going to go it alone, if necessary; but I knew I'd have a better chance with a partner who could at least see where we were going. One thing you'll find about me, son—I'm strictly practical."

"Doc," Tallon said wonderingly, "I love you."

The principal items in Winfield's escape kits were two large squares of thin tough plastic. He had stolen them from the Pavilion's receiving bay, where they had been used to cover bulk deliveries of food. His idea was to make a hole in the center, just big enough for a man's head, put it on, and working from the inside, seal the edges together with adhesive. Although crude, the envelopes provided a membrane area large enough to support a man's weight on the quagmire. In several years of steady filching, Winfield had accumulated a supply of antibiotics and specifics to fight any swamp fever and insect poison likely to be encountered. He even had a hypodermic syringe, two guard uniforms, and a small amount of money.

"The only thing I hadn't allowed for years ago," Winfield added, "is that our eyes will be traveling separately. I don't know how our feathered friends will make out in the swamp. Not too well, I'm afraid."

Tallon stroked the bird on his shoulder. "They'll have to have suits, too. If we go back to the workshop now, we can make up two small cages and cover them with transparent plastic. After that we should be ready to go whenever you say."

"I say tonight, then. There's no point in hanging around. I've wasted too much time, too many years in this place already, and I have a feeling that time's getting short for all of us."

As usual, the evening meal consisted of fish. In the two years he had been on the planet, Tallon had grown accustomed to having fish for nearly every meal; the sea was Emm Luther's only good source of first-class protein. Outside prison however, it was processed to taste like other things; in the Pavilion, fish tasted like fish.

Tallon toyed for a few minutes with the dry white flesh and the spinachlike sea vegetables, then rose and walked slowly out of the mess hall. He was finding it increasingly easy to get about in confined spaces using only an occasional glimpse of himself stolen from someone's eyes. Working through the bird—which he had named Ariadne— while it sat on his shoulder would have been better, but it would have drawn too much attention in the mess hall.

Winfield and he had decided to be as inconspicuous as possible during their last hours in the Pavilion. They had agreed to keep away from each other and make their way separately to the white rock at dusk, two hours before the cell blocks were sealed for the night. The doctor was to go first, carrying the improvised bird cages, and have the escape kits dug up by the time Tallon got there.

Outside the mess hall, Tallon stood undecidedly for a moment. There was almost an hour to go before it was rendezvous time. The only thing his stomach would have accepted at that moment was coffee, but Winfield had warned him not to eat or drink anything, because they were going to be sealed up in their plastic envelopes for at least two days. He touched the eyeset controls, and using proximity selection, got behind the eyes of a guard who was standing near the entrance. The guard was smoking, so Tallon lit a cigarette, and by raising it to his lips every time he saw the guard do likewise, he was able to achieve a startlingly realistic simulation of normal vision for a few minutes. He enjoyed re-creating a fragment of the warm, secure past. But gathering shadows behind the buildings around the plaza reminded him that night was falling over the swamp, and that he, Sam Tallon, would spend that night squirming through its stinking blackness toward the robot rifles.

Leaving the sounds of mealtime conversation and horseplay behind him, Tallon struck off across the square toward the cell blocks. The guard's eyes must have followed him idly, for Tallon had a perfect view of himself walking toward the blocks silhouetted on the western horizon. Self-consciously he squared his shoulders, but the action did nothing to make the receding figure seem any bigger, tougher, or less lonely.

He wanted to collect Ariadne from the large wire-mesh aviary, which the board had granted for the use of prisoners who wanted to keep bird pets, but decided to go to his cell first and clear out his possessions, such as they were. By the time Tallon reached his own section he was near the extreme range of the eyeset, and his view of himself was little more than of a brown speck approaching the entrance to the cell block. He thought he detected two other specks, wearing the dark green of the prison guards, detach themselves from the portico. The distance vision of the guard still smoking outside the mess hall was not very good, so Tallon decided to switch to a pair of eyes nearer to him.

As he raised his hands to the eyeset controls there was an impact of bodies, and his arms were pinned to his sides. Tallon saw that the green specks had attached themselves to the brown speck that was himself.

With his heart jolting violently, Tallon said, "If I've been reported for stealing cutlery from the mess hall, it's a lie."

"Don't try to be funny, Tallon," a voice crackled in his ear. "We want Winfield as well. Where is he?"

Tallon guessed that if they had not been able to find the doctor in the main buildings he must have already left for the rendezvous point. That meant Winfield might be able to get out of the Pavilion, if he didn't wait too long for Tallon to show up. But who had tipped off the guards? Not Hogarth, surely. Even if the little man had guessed what they were up to, he would hardly have . . .

"Do you not hear so good, Tallon? I asked you where Winfield was."

"I don't know." Tallon tried to think up a convincing stall to give the doctor more time, but his mind had gone numb. To his surprise, the guards did not seem to be particularly alarmed.

"What's the difference?" The man on his right spoke casually. "We'll collect this one now, and get Winfield's as soon as we see him."

"I guess that's all we can do."

As Tallon tried to make sense of their comments, he felt a hand brush his temple and, instantly, he was blind. They had taken his eyeset!

"What the hell!" He shouted angrily, wrenching his arms from their grasp and staggering slightly as the guards let go, leaving him free but helplessly blind.

"Give me that back. That's my own property, you thieving bastards. I'll report you to . . . Miss Juste for this."

One of the guards laughed. "That's a good one. You

52

and Winfield made these crazy glasses with stolen government materials, Tallon. And you can report us to Miss Juste any time you want. She's the one who's confiscating them."

nine

For a second the blunted needle refused to penetrate; then it punctured the skin and slid deep into Tallon's arm.

"Sorry, son," Winfield said. "I'm out of practice."

"Look, Doc, are you quite sure about all this? You made up a second escape kit so you could bring along somebody who could help you—not a blind man." Tallon rolled his sleeve down over his faintly throbbing arm.

"Sure I'm sure. Besides, I'm giving you this eyeset as soon as we're ready to move off."

"Nothing doing, Doc. You keep the eyeset and I'll stick with the sonar. I'm lucky to have that much, I suppose." Tallon had fallen several times during the nightmarish journey from the cell block to the meeting place, but had hardly felt the pain. His brain was trying to find the reason why Helen Juste had confiscated his eyeset. Why had she encouraged them to complete the eyesets before she cracked down? Had she got wind of their escape plan and chosen this way of slamming the door?

"Well, that's that," Winfield announced. "I wanted us to have the general-purpose shots before we started walking. Even the woodworms can have a nasty bite in this part of the world."

He pushed a bulky package into Tallon's arms, and they made their way cautiously down the slope toward the palisade. The bird on Winfield's shoulder clucked apprehensively as the doctor slid once on a patch of rank grass. Tallon kept the sonar torch aimed straight ahead and listened to the steadily rising tone caused by the beam hitting the palisade.

"Here we are," the doctor grunted. His voice was followed by dull crunching sounds as he kicked out the rotten wood inhabited by his carefully nurtured colony of worms. Tallon followed him through the hole, grimacing as an accidental contact with the edge showered him with thousands of tiny writhing creatures. They traveled a short

54

distance toward the swamp until they ran out of hard ground.

"Suits now," Winfield said brusquely. "Did you remember not to eat or drink?"

"Yes."

"Good, but you'd better have this anyway."

"What is it?"

"Diaper."

"You're kidding."

"You'll thank me for it later."

With Winfield doing most of the work, they draped the plastic sheets around their necks and sealed the edges. It was difficult to handle anything properly through the plastic, but Winfield produced a roll of adhesive tape and bound it at their necks, wrists and ankles. The binding made it possible for them to walk and move their arms with comparative freedom. To complete the grotesque outfits, they wrapped more plastic around their heads, finished it with cement and tape, then jammed on their prison caps.

"I'll carry the pack and the bird," Winfield said. "Stay as close to me as you can."

"You can count on that, Doc."

Moving toward the swamp in blackness, Tallon was aghast at the thought of what he was going to do. Although blind, he knew when he had reached the edge of the swamp by the feel of the clammy mist closing round him, as well as by the stench, which made every breath something to be planned in advance and forced through with determination. Unidentifiable night noises drifted through the swirling vapor, reminding him that, although the robot rifles had finished off only the swamp's warm-blooded inhabitants, there were others to share the darkness. And yet, Tallon was aware of feeling something approaching peace. He had finally become tired of drifting with the current, of compromising, of feeling afraid. The fat old doctor, with his head full of ridiculous dreams, was leading him to almost certain death; but he had taught Tallon one great truth: Walking toward death is not pleasant, but it's better than having it come up fast behind you.

The swamp was much worse than Tallon had anticipated; in fact, he discovered he had not really expected the swamp to be a problem. They were able to remain upright and move ahead by walking and wading for the first hour, covering about two hundred yards in reasonable comfort. But presently Tallon began to hit patches where his feet seemed to sink through six inches of molasses before reaching solid support. The goo made walking difficult but not impossible, even when it had begun to reach nearly to his knees. Tallon went steadily ahead, sweating in his plastic sheet. Then the bottom seemed to drop out of the world. Instead of his feet finding bedrock, they kept going down and down as though the whole planet was sucking him through its skin.

"Fall forward," Winfield shouted. "Throw yourself down on it and keep your arms spread out."

Tallon splashed forward, spread-eagled on the heaving surface of the quagmire, embracing its filth. The water splashed over his face, and sediment swirled to the surface, releasing all the odors of death. Uncontrollable spasms of retching forced his face down again, into the crawling fluid.

"Are you all right, son?" Winfield's voice was anxious.

Tallon's first impulse was to shout for help in his black, blind universe, but he clenched his teeth and kept beating the surface of the quagmire with his arms. Gradually his feet worked upward, and he moved forward again in a semiswimming motion.

"I'm all right, Doc. Keep traveling."

"That's the way. It won't all be like this."

Furious splashing sounds from up ahead told Tallon the doctor was already moving on. Grinning with desperation, Tallon flailed after him. Sometimes they would reach little islands where they were able to travel short distances on foot, beating their way through the rubbery vegetation. At other times they encountered solid curtains of vines and had to go to the side or even backtrack to get by them. Once Tallon put his hand squarely on something lying flat and icy smooth below the surface. It humped convulsively and drove out from under his body with silent strength, paralyzing him with fear.

As the night wore on Tallon found himself catching up to Winfield with increasing frequency, and he realized the doctor was reaching the point of exhaustion. Winfield's breathing became a harsh, monotonous sobbing.

"Listen, Doc," Tallon finally shouted. "We both need a rest. Is there any point in risking a heart attack?"

"Keep moving. There's nothing wrong with my heart."

Tallon found some firm ground under his feet. He lunged forward, throwing his weight onto Winfield, and brought him crashing down. The doctor fought him off stubbornly while struggling to move on.

"For Christ's sake, Doc," Tallon gasped, "I'm talking about *my* heart. Take it easy, will you?"

Winfield fought on for a moment, then went limp. "Okay, son," he said between gasps. "I'll give you five minutes."

"Believe me, Doc, I'm grateful to you."

"I'm grateful to myself."

They lay huddled together, laughing weakly while Winfield's breathing gradually returned to normal. Tallon told him of his encounter with the underwater creature.

"A slinker—harmless at this time of the year," Winfield said. "In the laying season, though, the skin of the female toughens into knife edges at the sides. They slice past anything that moves, laying it open, and inject their eggs at the same time."

"Nice habits."

"Yes. I'm told the thing to do is to think of it not as losing a foot, but as gaining a batch of slinker offspring. As a matter of fact, we're making this trip at a very good time. The swamp is pretty quiet late on in the winter. The only real danger is from muck spiders."

"Poisonous?"

"No. With the sort of mouths they have, poison would be superfluous. They lie in shallow water, with their legs stuck up in the air like bullrushes, and there's nothing in the middle but mouth. If you ever come through here again, son, avoid walking through any neat circular clumps of bullrushes."

Tallon got an unpleasant idea. "What's that bird's night vision like? Are you getting a good enough picture to let you spot a muck spider?"

Winfield snorted. "What are you worrying about? Aren't I going first?"

When daylight came to the swamp Winfield insisted on letting Tallon have a spell with the eyeset.

Tallon accepted, grateful for the release from blackness, and took the lead for several hours. He used a crude spear, which Winfield had made by snapping a thin sapling, to beat smaller vegetation out of his way. The bird fluttered occasionally in its plastic-covered cage, but showed no signs of any real discomfort. As he moved through slow-dripping foliage Tallon saw that the water was alive with dark brown leechlike creatures, writhing, twisting, continually warring on each other. Great streamers of their dark bodies trailed around his legs. The air hummed with the vibration of tiny gnats, or was parted by the heavy throb of huge sooty-black insects blundering through the swamp, intent on unknown missions.

Twice during the day, low-flying aircraft swept by directly overhead, but the ice-green mist hid them from view. Tallon's mental processes slowed down while he labored mechanically, thinking river-bed thoughts, dreaming brown dreams. Their rest periods grew longer, and the intervals between them shorter, as fatigue spread through their bodies. At dusk they found a small knoll of almost dry ground and slept like children.

The robot rifles were more than capable of shooting clear across the four-mile reach of swamp, so their missiles were fitted with time fuses, which limited the range to two thousand yards. Their effective range, however, was governed by the density of the swamp mist. When it was at its thickest a man could get within four hundred yards of the pylons before his body heat reached the trigger threshold. But even in the murkiest periods, a sudden gust of wind could open a swirling avenue far into the swamp, the gleaming grasshopper legs of the servos would contract, and a heavy slug would howl its way down the misty tree lanes.

Winfield had thought a lot about the rattler rifles while he was planning his escape.

On the second morning in the swamp he opened his pack, took out a small knife, and split the plastic that covered Tallon's hands and his own. They gathered armfuls of the thick, double-walled *dringo* leaves, dodging the whizzing leaps of the sheltering scorpions, and sewed them together to make heavy dark green blankets.

"We'll soon be back on dry land," Winfield said. "You can see the green stuff thinning out already. The mist is quite heavy this morning, so we're all right for another few hundred yards; but after that keep your head down and stay under your screen. Got it?"

"Keep my head down and stay under my screen."

The encumbrance of the heavy blanket of leaves made movement more difficult than ever. Tallon sweltered under the plastic as he struggled along behind the doctor, deprived of even the meager companionship of the sonar torch's electronic voice in his ear. He had had to switch it off as soon as the screen was pulled over his head.

They inched their way forward for two hours before Tallon noticed that the going was getting easier. Gradually there was less backtracking to do, fewer floundering escapes from seemingly bottomless wells of slime. He began to think about the possibility of walking upright in fresh air, of being clean and dry, of eating again. . . .

Suddenly, up ahead, Winfield gave a hoarse scream.

"Doc! What is it?" Tallon heard violent splashing sounds, and cursed his blind helplessness. "What's wrong, Doc?"

"A spider. A big one. . . ." The doctor screamed again, and the splashing grew louder.

Tallon threw aside the burden of leaves and crept forward as quickly as he could, expecting at any moment to put his unprotected hand far down into a cold wet mouth.

"Where are you, Doc? Can you see me?"

"This way, son. That's far enough. Hold out your . . . left hand."

Tallon did as he was told and felt something light and brittle drop into his fingers. It was the eyeset. He put it on and was jolted with green blurs of brilliant light. Winfield had dropped the birdcage, and Tallon found himself looking at an unearthly scene through the slime-streaked plastic. At first he did not recognize the mud-splattered starfish shape that was himself or the other writhing one that was Winfield.

The doctor was lying on his back, and his right leg was sunk up to the knee in a seething patch of turbulence. Red stains were spreading in the churning water, and around its perimeter eight jointed stalks whipped and quivered in the air. Moaning with dismay, Tallon oriented himself and lunged sideways for the spear, which had dropped clear of Winfield's hand. He lifted it and drove the point down through the mud toward where he guessed the muck spider's body to be. The surface of the water heaved sluggishly, and the spear twisted in his grasp.

"Hold on, Doc. I'm using the spear on it."

"It won't work that way. Skin too tough. Got—got to go down the throat. Give me the spear."

Tallon hauled the spear back and guided it into Winfield's blindly grasping hand. The doctor's mouth gaped silently as he took the crude weapon and worked the point down into the water close to his leg. The green stalks clawed eagerly at his arms, then suddenly sprang upright.

"I'm getting there," Winfield grunted. "I'm getting it."

He grasped the spear higher up on its shaft and triumphantly began to go up it, hand over hand. The surface of the swamp all around him convulsed as his weight bore down on the vibrating spear. Tallon, crouched close by, was totally absorbed in the struggle when silent alarms began to sound in his head. Winfield was winning his battle, but there was another danger, something they were forgetting.

"Doc!" he shouted. *You're standing up!*

59

Winfield froze for an instant, looking guilty rather than afraid, and was dropping to the ground when the missile claimed him.

Tallon heard the incredible impact, the subway roar of the missile's flight arriving in its wake, and he glimpsed the doctor's headless body cartwheeling away over the water. Seconds later came the tardy, rolling echoes of the rifle shot. The spear still stood upright in the mud, rocking slightly with the movements of the unseen spider.

That was a stupid action, Tallon thought numbly; you weren't supposed to stand up, Doc. You warned me not to stand up, and then *you* stood up. He crouched on his hands and knees for several seconds, shaking his head bewilderedly; then the anger returned, the same anger that had let him carry Cherkassky out through a hotel window into the thin air high above New Wittenburg.

Tallon wiped the slime off the plastic cover of the bird cage to give himself a better view of his own actions; then he crept to the spear. Ignoring the beating of the jointed green stalks, he pulled the spear up and drove it back down into the same spot again and again, until the water was whorled with cream-colored fluid. Pulling the spear up for the last time, he went in search of Winfield's body. He found it in a shallow pool, already shrouded in a shimmering cloak of leeches.

"I'm sorry, Doc," he said aloud, "but Earth expects you to do one more thing. And I know you would want to oblige."

Tallon worked the tip of the spear into a fold in the plastic of the doctor's suit, and groaning with the effort, levered the body into an upright position. He was much closer this time, and the impact of the second missile stunned his senses as the spear and its grisly burden were ripped from his fingers. Tallon collected the bird and the supply pack, then draped himself in the heavy screen of *dringo* leaves. He moved forward for another four hours before he risked making a tiny opening in the overlapping leaves and holding the bird cage close to it.

He had almost reached the northern edge of the swamp, and far ahead, with sunlight gleaming on its upper surfaces, the slim pylon of a rattler rifle soared up above the mists. Tallon had no way of knowing if he was looking at the rifle that had killed Logan Winfield, but somewhere along the line one of the sentient machines would be registering two missiles fired. To the Pavilion security force, two missiles fired would mean that two prisoners had terminated their sentences.

Beyond the slender pylon Tallon glimpsed the sloping

gray uplands of the continent's spinal ridge. He settled down, with the bird cage held tight in his arms, to wait for night and the start of the real journey.

There were still a thousand miles to New Wittenburg —and eighty thousand portals to Earth.

ten

Tallon passed through the line of pylons at dusk.

He guessed the declination of the rifles would be limited to the edge of the swamp and beyond, but he stayed beneath the screen anyway, and the crawling feeling between his shoulder blades remained there until he had safely crossed the line. His first action on the other side was to cut away the plastic envelope, wrap it inside the leaves, and hide the bundle in a clump of prickly shrub. Working quickly, he took Ariadne II out of her cage, tied her leg to the epaulette of his prison uniform, and climbed the palisade that kept the general public from straying into the rattlers' domain.

The exhilaration of freedom, of walking like a human being on firm ground again, sustained Tallon as he moved diagonally over the rocky foothills marking the beginning of a mountain chain that straggled the whole length of the continent. When he had gained a little height he saw the trembling, varicolored lights of a small town clustered in the curve of a bay about five miles distant. The awesome planetary ocean stretched blackly away to the west, pricked here and there by the navigation lights of trawlers. He breathed deeply, savoring his release from the Pavilion, as well as the release from all pressures of human identity—a feeling one gets when nobody in the whole universe knows where he is or even if he exists.

At that moment the journey Tallon was about to attempt seemed absurdly easy. This, had he lived, would have been Winfield's hour of triumph, Tallon knew. But the doctor was dead, and dead again.

Suddenly Tallon was tired and hungry and aware that he stank. There were no lights visible between him and the town—the ground appeared too rough for any sort of farming—so he headed down again to the water's edge. On the way he searched in Winfield's pack and found, in addition to the green guards' uniforms, a flashlight, soap, and depilatory cream. There were also several bars of candy—more reminders of the old doctor's years of patient work toward a day he was never going to see.

Standing on the pebbles of the narrow beach, Tallon stripped and washed in the cold sea. Keeping only his boots, he put on the fresh clothing and was relieved to find that one of the stretch-fabric uniforms fit him well enough. He tied the unprotesting bird to one shoulder, slung the pack over the other, and began walking north.

At first it seemed a good idea to stick to the beach in preference to the rock-strewn hillside, but as he walked it became obvious that there was no real beach. Mostly there was just a tiny strip of rough pebbles, and in many places tough grasses grew right to the water's edge. After he'd been stumbling along the uneven stones for a while Tallon remembered he was not going to find any stretches of smooth sand. Emm Luther had no moon, which meant it had practically no tides, and therefore no beaches and no sand.

If only there were a moon, darling, we could have a moonlit picnic on the beach, he thought, *if only there were a beach.*

Munching the candy, he moved a little farther inland, with the intention of walking until he was perhaps half a mile from the town, and then trying to get some rest; but an unexpected occurrence forced him to change his plans. Ariadne II went to sleep. Tallon flicked the bird with his finger a few times, and she opened her eyes for a couple of seconds, but closed them again, plunging him into darkness. He felt annoyed, but this soon passed when he considered what she had been through on his behalf. In all probability any Earthside species of bird would have died from overadrenalation long before this.

He lay down and tried to sleep. Although he was almost as far south as it was possible to go on Emm Luther and still remain on dry land, winter was just beginning to blend into spring and the night was cold. A long time went by before he achieved unconsciousness, and then he had dreams—of talking to Winfield, of dancing with Helen Juste, of flying up and up into the coppery light of dawn with the long-shadowed land falling away below. This last was very vivid. There was a tiny figure of a man in a dark green uniform lying down there on the grass. Tallon moved, clutching frantically for support. *He was flying!* Horizons of sea and land rotated sickeningly, and there was nothing under him but air.

His fingers sank into wiry grass. He became aware of the pressure of the hard ground against his back, and came fully awake. The visions of wheeling land and sea persisted, but now he knew what was causing them. Ariadne II had worked herself free and had escaped while she had the chance. The pictures grayed out as she passed beyond the range of the eyeset.

Her loss presented him with another problem—finding new eyes and using them to get hold of some food. He had to get something solid to eat in a hurry. The candy had given his blood sugar a temporary boost, but the overstimulation of the pancreas, which always accompanies the intake of neat carbohydrate, had flooded his system with sugar-annihilating insulin. The result was that his blood sugar had dropped even farther below the fasting level, and now he could hardly stand without his knees buckling. He wished the doctor had thought enough about the nutrition problems of a blind man on the run to have included milk solids or some other convenient form of protein in the escape kit. But that was not getting him any closer to the space terminal at New Wittenburg.

Tallon put the eyeset on "search and hold" and picked up seabirds cruising over the water near the shore. He got more aerial views of the ocean dressed in its early morning grays, the tousled hillside, and his own dark green figure. This was good enough to let him continue walking north. It was still very early in the morning, and he reached the outskirts of the town just as the place was coming awake. He was able to switch to the eyes of men driving to work at dawn. None of them seemed to pay attention to him.

For a while Tallon was content to walk free along the quiet thoroughfares, marveling at how Earth-like his surroundings were. The big northern city of Testament, where he had spent most of his time while on Emm Luther, had a character of its own that was unlike anything on Earth; but small towns were small towns no matter where you went in the galaxy. The neat bungalows, sleeping in the morning stillness, were the same as those he had seen on half a dozen worlds; and the children's tricycles, lying on the front lawns, were painted red, because human children the galaxy over liked them that way.

Why should a man choose one planet and say, this one I will put above all others? If he survived the psychic disembowelment of the flicker-transits and arrived on yet another miraculous green orb, why shouldn't that be enough? Why carry with him the paraphernalia of political allegiances, doctrinal conflicts, imperialism, the Block?

And yet Winfield had been blown to bits, and Sam Tallon was still carrying the location of a brand-new planet embedded in his brain.

He found a diner and spent a tenth of his money on a huge platter of fish steaks and sea greens, which he washed down with four cups of coffee. Neither the elderly waitress who served him, nor the one other customer— whose eyes Tallon was using—glanced at him twice. He reckoned he could have been taken for anything from a TV repairman to an employee of an obscure section of the local utilities complex.

Out in the street again he bought a pack of cigarettes from a vendor and walked along casually, smoking, pretending to look into store windows any time he lost sight of himself. More people were about, and he found it relatively easy to skip to fresh eyes and spot himself quickly from the new viewpoint. He discovered that very few people had perfect eyesight. The eyes he borrowed as he crossed the town were often nearsighted or farsighted, astigmatic or color blind, and he was mildly surprised to find that the people with the most defective vision were often the ones who did not wear glasses.

Many of the large downtown buildings were fronted with 3-D screens displaying shifting color patterns keyed to the tonal patterns of current music. There was no advertising, but a video newscast was put on every fifteen minutes or so. Tallon was too concerned with the second-by-second problems of negotiating crowds and crossing streets to pay much attention to the news, but his attention was suddenly gripped by a huge picture of a dovelike bird perched on a man's finger. A piece of string dangled from one of its legs. Tallon was sure it was Ariadne II. He strained to hear the commentary.

. . . . *arrived back at the Government Detention Center early this morning. It is believed the two sightless detainees were carrying the bird with them, and its return is another indication that they perished in the swamp. Earlier reports that the two men had obtained radarlike devices to take the place of normal eyes have since been denied by a spokesman for the Center.*

And now, passing from the local scene to the galactic situation, the Moderator's delegates to the prematurely ended top-level conference on Akkab will arrive at the New Wittenburg space terminal this afternoon. It is understood . . .

Tallon moved on, frowning. It was good to know that he was presumed dead and therefore wouldn't be hunted, but the newscast had stirred up in his mind the mystery of

Helen Juste. Was she in trouble with the prison board for her unorthodoxy? Had she seen the trouble coming and tried to avoid it by ordering the confiscation of the eyesets? Why had she let them go so far in the first place?

A sign attached to the façade of the central post office confirmed Tallon's guess that he was in the town of Sirocco. His hazy memory of Lutheran geography told him that Sirocco was on the continuous railway that circled the whole continent, performing the function of air services on other worlds. Winfield's plan had been to travel at night and on foot, which had been reasonable enough, considering the limitations of the sonar torch; but Tallon could actually see. And apart from what appeared to be a rather heavy pair of spectacles, he looked much like any other citizen of Emm Luther. If he took the train he could be back in New Wittenburg in little more than a day. Once there, he would be faced with the difficulty of making contact with an agent, but it would be better to face the problem sooner than later. The alternative to the train was to start walking and run all the risks of having to live by stealing food, sleeping in sheds and barns, and in general acting in a highly suspicious manner. He decided to take the train.

As he walked he passed the time by practicing lip reading, an ability taught by the Block, and one for which he had never found much practical use. The recurring close-ups of faces of persons talking without the accompanying sound effects presented a challenge to Tallon. He wanted to find out what they were saying.

Tallon had often heard of the continuous railway, and in his cover job as an agent for Earth-made drafting systems he had even used it for shipping goods, but he had never seen it.

Arriving at the station, he saw a slow-moving line of carriages going by the long single platform and assumed he had got there just as a train was moving off or stopping. The railway operated on a universal fare system, so there were no formalities over tickets. A machine provided him with a simple square of plastic entitling him to travel anywhere on the southern section for one day. He worked through knots of people and piles of freight onto the platform and stood waiting for the quietly drifting carriages to either speed up or finally come to a halt. Five minutes passed before he realized that neither of these things was going to happen; the railway really was continuous!

Tallon flicked the eyeset controls several times until he picked up a better view of the station and the system. The

66

composite picture he built up showed an endless line of freight and passenger cars curving into the station from the east and vanishing to the north. None of the cars had an engine or any visible controls, yet they were moving quickly beyond the station and slowing down to about three miles an hour as they came alongside the platform. This puzzled him, till he saw that what he had taken to be a third rail was, in fact, a rotating screw mounted centrally between the wheel-bearing rails. It was then he began to appreciate the beauty of the system.

The cars needed no engines because their power came from the central screw, which was turned at a constant speed by small magnetic motors spaced about every half mile. Each car was attached to what amounted to an ordinary nut, which was pulled along by the action of the spinning screw. The cars needed no controls because their forward speed was governed by a device whose simplicity pleased the engineer in Tallon: where they approached the station, the pitch of the threads on the central screw was greatly reduced. This had the effect of automatically slowing them down to walking pace.

Momentarily bemused by his admiration for Emm Luther's practical engineering, Tallon blended with a group of teen-age students who were waiting for the next passenger car to come by. He was looking through the eyes of a station official standing behind the group. As the car came close he moved toward it with the chattering students, then discovered he had overlooked an important feature of the continuous railway. The edge of the platform was a slideway moving at the same speed as the train, to let people get on and off safely.

Tallon's right foot moved out from under him as he surged forward with the students, and he lurched sideways, completely off balance. There were startled protests as he grabbed for support and then fell awkwardly into the carriage, hitting the side of his head on the door frame.

Apologizing profusely, he dropped into an empty seat, hoping he had not been so conspicuous as to make anyone look closely at him. His right ear was throbbing hotly, but the pain was a secondary consideration. The blow from the door post had fallen directly on the part of the eyeset's frame that concealed the miniature power pack, and Tallon thought he had experienced a brief grayout at the moment of impact. He was still receiving vision from the station official back on the platform, so he reselected on proximity, and got one of the students who had sat down on the opposite side of the compartment. After a moment Tallon relaxed; the eyeset seemed to be undamaged, and the other passengers apparently had forgotten his spectacular entrance.

The carriage gradually gathered speed until it was doing a smooth forty miles an hour in almost complete silence. The route northward kept close to the ocean. Occasionally the mountains on the other side receded to a distance of up to ten miles, but usually they were crowding in, limiting the living space, creating the pressures that were being felt back on Earth. The ribbon of flatland was a continuous suburban development, with commercial centers every few miles. A break in the continental spine became visible after half an hour, and another similiar train, going in the opposite direction, slid into place beside the one on which Tallon was traveling. He saw that at top speed the few feet of space that separated the cars at a station multiplied in the same ratio as the cars' speed, so that they were quite widely strung out.

The students got out at one of the urban ganglia, but there was a continuous supply of other passengers to keep him provided with borrowed eyes. He noticed the women were more attractively dressed and more sophisticated than was usual in the colder north where the austere influence of Reformation, the governmental seat, was stronger. Some of the girls were wearing the new visi-perfumes, which surrounded them in pastel-tinted clouds of fragrance.

Once he used the eyes of a young woman who, judging by the way Tallon kept seeing himself in the center of his field of vision, was showing some interest in him. He flicked to another pair of eyes a few seats away and got a look at the woman. After noting that she had a bronzed, blond attractiveness Tallon, with the comfortable feeling of successful cheating, went back to her eyes to find out just how much she was interested by the number of times she looked at him.

Soothed by the movement of the carriage, the sun-lit warmth, the very presence of women, Tallon felt the first stirrings of sexuality that he had experienced in a long, long time. How good it would be, he thought drowsily, to be living normally again, to be swimming with the warm currents of life, to have a woman with red hair and whiskey-colored eyes. ...

Tallon turned off his eyeset, and slept. He awoke to the persistent chiming of the public address system, and switched on the eyeset again. A man's voice announced that the carriage was about to reach the city of Sweetwell, the northernmost point of the section, and would then be swinging to the east. Any passengers who wished to continue traveling north would have to get off and cross the Vajda Strait on the ferry. They would be able to board the central section train on the other side.

Tallon had forgotten that the bottom of the continent was separated from the rest by a narrow incursion of the sea. He began to swear silently, and was immediately astonished at the change in his attitude a few hours of comfort and safety had brought about. Last night he had been prepared to crawl to New Wittenburg on his hands and knees if necessary; today he was annoyed at having to change trains on the journey.

He stretched, and seeing himself perform the familiar action, realized that the blond girl was still opposite him and still showing interest. He turned his face until he seemed to be looking directly into his own eyes and smiled his best smile. The picture of himself looking pale and haggard, perhaps romantically so, remained for a few seconds before the girl's gaze slid away to the passing buildings outside the train. He guessed she had smiled back at him for a moment, and he was warmed.

Tallon stood up as the platform came alongside; the man nearest the compartment door slid it open. The girl rose at the same time, and he knew she was smiling at him again. Outside, the platform was drifting by, and it was now imperative for Tallon to get off without falling. He had automatically motioned the girl to go ahead of him, then remembered that if she did he would be out of her field of vision.

"Sorry, miss," he muttered regretfully, and elbowed past her to the door. She gasped, but his sudden rudeness had the useful effect of fixing her gaze firmly on his back. He got down onto the slideway and stepped safely on to the stationary platform. The girl continued to shoot angry glances at him when she was off the train, and until she was out of range he used her attention to guide him to the waiting ferry. It was about noon and the day was brilliantly clear. He was hungry again and decided to treat himself to a huge meal on the far side of the Strait, regardless of the cost. At his present rate of progress his money would be more than adequate.

The ferry turned out to be a primitive but fast ground effect machine, capable of crossing the mile-wide Strait in a couple of minutes. Tallon found the short trip exhilarating. The characteristic yawing ride of the hovercraft, the roar of the turbines, white spray flying on each side, the jostling of the other travelers in the stand-up passenger saloon—all combined to produce a cheerful vacation mood. The vessel waltzed up its ramp and into the dock. Tallon strolled through the group of people waiting to embark, and began looking for a good restaurant. There was a diner attached to the rail terminal complex, but it looked slightly squalid, and he had no doubt it would charge high prices for indifferent food.

He walked up sloping streets toward the center of city still enjoying the sense of freedom. Sweetwell was a bustling city with a suggestion of provincial France in its sophisticated little stores and sidewalk cafes. He would have enjoyed eating in the sunlight, but decided not to throw away all caution—his picture was bound to have been included in the newscasts and there was always the chance that somebody might look too closely at him and start wondering. Accordingly he picked a quiet restaurant, with a Gothic sign identifying it as The Persian Cat.

The only other customers were two pairs of middle-aged women sipping coffee and smoking, with shopping bags on the floor at their feet. Tallon flicked the eyeset, got behind the eyes of one of the women, and saw himself walk in and sit down at a vacant table. The tables were of real wood and were covered with what seemed to be genuine linen. Two large gray cats padded about among the chair legs. Tallon, who was not a cat enthusiast, shifted uneasily and wished one of the other customers would look at a menu.

The food, when he finally got it, was quite good. The steak had been processed so well that Tallon could not detect the taste of fish at all, and he guessed it would cost him plenty. He ate quickly, suddenly impatient to be back on the train, gulped the coffee, and reached for his money.

His wallet was gone.

Tallon searched his other pockets mechanically, knowing all the while that his wallet had been stolen, probably during the jostling ride across the Strait. The ferry was an obvious hunting ground for pickpockets, and Tallon swore at his own carelessness. The situation was serious, for he was now in trouble with the restaurant and could not buy a train ticket later.

Toying with the dregs of his coffee, Tallon decided that if he was going to start stealing money The Persian Cat was as good a place as any to do it. It seemed to have only one afternoon waitress, who spent long periods out in the kitchen, leaving the cash desk near the door unattended. It was a foolishly trusting thing to do, he thought; almost as foolish as not holding on to your wallet in a crowd.

Two of the middle-aged shoppers were still in the restaurant. Waiting for them to leave, Tallon motioned to one of the gray cats and lured it over to him. He lifted the heavy animal onto his lap, trying to tickle it behind the ears, and adjusted the eyeset to put him behind its great yellow eyes.

Tallon feared the other two customers were going to stay until somebody else came in and ruined his chance, but they finally gathered up the shopping and rang for their check. To Tallon's surprise it was not the waitress who had served him who emerged from the screen at the rear; it was instead a tall brunette of about thirty, wearing black-rimmed glasses and an expensively tailored business suit. He decided she was either the manager or the owner.

One her way back from the cash desk the brunette stopped at his table. He raised the almost empty coffee cup to his lips.

"Can I get you anything more?"

Tallon shook his head. "Nothing, thanks. I'm enjoying your excellent coffee."

"I see you like my cats."

"Love them," Tallon lied. "Beautiful creatures. This is a particularly fine cat. What's his name?"

"His name is Ethel."

Tallon smirked desperately, wondering if real cat lovers were supposed to be able to tell toms from tabbies at a glance. He concentrated on stroking Ethel's head, and the brunette, after giving him a suspicious look, moved off toward the screen. The little encounter had filled Tallon with a sense of uneasiness, and he decided to waste no more time. He held the cat up and rotated it, making sure the restaurant was deserted, then walked quickly to the desk. The old-fashioned cash register was bound to make a noise when he operated it, so Tallon edged the door open slightly in preparation for a quick escape. He pressed a key on the register and feverishly scooped a handful of bills from the drawer.

"Detainee Samuel Tallon," a woman's voice said softly behind him.

Tallon spun, with the cat under his arm, and saw the

expensively dressed brunette. Her eyes, behind the black-rimmed glasses, had a hard speculative glint in them. She was aiming a gold-plated automatic pistol squarely at his chest.

eleven

Tallon lay on the bed, in utter blackness, listening to night sounds and waiting for Amanda Weisner to come for him.

Beside him on the scented silks his dog, Seymour, snuffled and growled in his sleep, stirring slightly from time to time. Tallon stroked the terrier's rough hair, feeling the warmth in the compact little body, and was glad he had insisted on having the dog in spite of Amanda's objections. He reached for his cigarettes, then changed his mind. There was something unsatisfactory about a cigarette unless he could actually see the smoke and the tiny red ash. He could have wakened Seymour to borrow his eyes, but that seemed inconsiderate.

Apart from Seymour's feelings, there were practical reasons for not using the eyeset at night. The original suggestion had been Amanda's, but he had decided to go along with it because it meant a reduced demand on the power pack. Twice during his first week at The Persian Cat there had been momentary grayouts similar to the one that had occurred when he hit his head on the train. There had been no more since he had begun resting the eyeset, so he considered the nightly return to blindness worth the inconvenience.

He heard the rear door of the restaurant downstairs open and close again. That meant Amanda was putting the cats out for the night and would soon be coming to bed. *Their* bed. Tallon clenched his fist and pressed the knuckles hard against his teeth.

When he'd seen the pistol that first day he thought his luck was gone; then when he learned Amanda was not going to turn him over to the E.L.S.P. he decided it was back again. After he got to know Amanda better he realized he had been right the first time.

She had square-jawed good looks, in which a slight masculinity was accentuated by cropped dark hair and heavy spectacles. Her body had a snaky, economical beauty, but it was Amanda Weisner's mind that fascinated

73

Tallon. Although there had been frequent sexual encounters during that first week, he sensed these were unimportant to her. Mentally, however, she had devoured him.

The question and answer sessions went on for hours, covering every detail of his previous career, his life in the Pavilion, the escape. Her memory was extremely good, seemingly capable of filing and cross-indexing each fact, so that sooner or later every lie and honest error in his answers was uncovered and pinned down.

Tallon could not understand what was driving her; he only knew as they lay together talking far into the night that he was once more in a prison.

She never actually threatened him with the police, not in so many words, but she left no doubt as to his position. In two weeks he had not been outside the restaurant once, nor even beyond the door of Amanda's flat. Seymour was the only concession Tallon had won, and that only at the end of a major clash of wills. She had offered him one of her eight cats to use as eyes, and had smiled whitely when he said he hated cats.

"I know you do, Sam," she said caressingly. "How do you think I noticed you so quickly when you came into the restaurant? I don't know who was the most on edge that day—you or Ethel. Cat people aren't so easily fooled."

"You mean," Tallon muttered, "it takes one to spot one."

Amanda had given him a cold, level stare at that, and when she finally brought him the wire-haired terrier she hinted she could not be responsible for its safety in the presence of her cats. Tallon had accepted the dog gratefully, and revealing a latent weakness for puns, christened it Seymour. Since then, the number one stud on the eyeset had been permanently allocated to the dog.

The eyeset had fascinated Amanda. She had gone as far as she could with him in understanding its design principles, and had even tried it out for herself, making him do without it for hours while she explored the world of her cat family. When she closed her eyes the set worked quite well for her, except that she occasionally lost the picture through not having metal plugs in her corneas to act as focusing referents. Tallon had been forced to sit, helplessly blind, as she lay on the floor wearing the eyeset. He heard the whispering sounds as her long body coiled and uncoiled ecstatically on the thick carpets, tiny cat noises issuing from her slim throat. And all he could do was clench his fist and press the knuckles hard against his teeth. . . .

The bedroom door opened and he heard Amanda come in.

"Sleeping already, darling?"

"Not yet. I'm working on it, though."

Tallon listened to the faint crackling of static electricity in her clothing as she undressed. If only she would let one night go by without the intolerable demands of love where love did not exist, the relationship might be bearable. She was more intense, more insistent than ever since he had begun his nightly return to blindness. He guessed it was because his helplessness without the eyeset satisfied some psychological need in her.

"Darling, have you that filthy dog beside you again?"

"Seymour isn't filthy."

"If you say so, darling; but should he be on our bed?"

Tallon sighed as he set the dog on the floor. "I like having Seymour around. Don't I have any privileges around this place?"

"What privileges had you in the Center, darling?"

Point taken, Tallon thought. How had he done it? How, out of a million or more inhabitants in the city of Sweetwell, had he unerringly picked out Amanda Weisner? But then, he reflected somberly, Sam Tallon had always found the Amandas everywhere he went. How had he started out as a physicist and ended up working for the Block? How, out of all the safe jobs that were available, had he selected the one that placed him so precisely in the wrong place at the wrong time?

The night was very warm, as spring had come early to the southern end of the long continent. As the hours went by Tallon tried to free himself from the physical duel with Amanda by letting his mind drift upward, through ceiling and roof, to where he would be able to see the slow wheeling of alien constellations. Out in the alley behind the restaurant the big cats prowled and pounced, just as their ancestors on Earth had always done, telling each other wailing cat myths to explain the absence of the moon, which had gilded their eyes for a thousand centuries.

Occasionally there were sharper cries as male and female came together savagely, obeying an instinct older than the moon and as universal as matter. Tallon slowly realized that, time after time, Amanda's body was responding to the ferocious outbursts, and he felt his mind borne away on powerful tides of disgust. If he walked out on her she would go to the police—of that he was certain. He could kill her, except for the fact that her daily employees in the restaurant would notice her absence within a matter of hours. And yet he had to consider the possibility that she could soon grow bored with him and turn him over no matter what he did.

Moving restlessly in the darkness, Tallon brushed Amanda's face with his hand and touched the smoothness of plastic, the edges of tiny projections. Immediately both their bodies were stilled.

"What was that?" He kept his voice low to mask the cold dawning in his mind.

"What was what, darling? You mean my silly old glasses? I had forgotten I was wearing them."

Tallon considered the words for a moment, pretending to relax, then he snatched the eyeset from her face and put it to his own. He got one glimpse of the night jungle through which the big cats moved, before the eyeset was torn away from him again.

Mewing with rage, Amanda attacked, using nails and teeth as naturally and efficiently as would one of her cats. Tallon was handicapped both by his blindness and by his alarm at the thought of accidentally smashing the eyeset, which had dropped on the bed beside them.

Stoically enduring the tearing of his skin, he groped for the eyeset and placed it safely under the bed. He then subdued Amanda by holding her throat with his left hand and driving slow, rhythmic punches into her face with his right. Even when she had gone limp he kept hitting her, seeking revenge for things he barely understood.

Ten minutes later Tallon opened the front door of The Persian Cat and stepped out onto the street. He walked quickly, with the freshly filled pack bumping solidly against his back and Seymour wriggling sleepily under his arm. There were about five hours of darkness left in which he could travel northward, but he had a feeling the hunt would start long before daylight.

twelve

Tallon was clearing the outskirts of the city when he heard the lonely clattering of a single helicopter. Its navigation lights drifted across the sky, high up in the predawn grayness. In a technology that had learned to negate gravity itself, the helicopter was a crude contraption, but it was still the most efficient vertical-takeoff machine ever devised, and it was unlikely to go out of use as long as some men had to run and others had to hunt them like eagles.

Holding Seymour's head upright, Tallon watched the solitary light drift out of sight beyond the northern horizon. Amanda had wasted no time, he thought. Now that any glimmer of hope of not being reported to the police was gone he began looking for a safe place to wait out the coming day. He was walking on a second-class motorway, lined on one side with native trees and on the other with stunted palms grown in the higher gravity of Emm Luther from imported seeds. At that time of the morning traffic was limited to infrequent private automobiles, traveling fast, trailing turbulent wakes of dust and dried leaves.

Tallon kept close to the trees, hiding each time he saw headlights, and scanned the quiet buildings for a likely place to sleep. As he left Sweetwell behind, the neat garden factories were gradually replaced by small flatblocks, and then by private houses in the higher income class. The tailored lawns shone in the light from the motorway. Several times as he walked, his view of his surroundings seemed to dim slightly, and he whispered fiercely to Seymour, urging the terrier to alertness. But in the end he had to admit to himself that the fault was in the eyeset. He fingered the tiny slide controlling the gain and was shocked to discover it was almost up against the end of its slot. It looked as though the damage he had done to the power unit was progressive in effect, in which case . . .

Tallon dismissed the thought and concentrated on finding a place to spend the day. Lights were beginning to appear in windows as he opened the door of a shrub-covered shed behind one of the larger dwellings. The darkness in the shed was filled with the nostalgic odor of dry earth, garden tools, and machine oil. Tallon settled down in a corner, with Seymour, and sorted out some of his new possessions. He had Amanda Weisner's gold-plated automatic, enough food for several days, a roll of bills, and a radio. Later in the day as he lay in his private universe of blackness, with the eyeset switched off, he was able to pick up the first newcasts.

Detainee Samuel Tallon, he learned, was still alive and had reached the city of Sweetwell. Tallon, who had been convicted of spying for imperialist Earth, had forced his way into a Sweetwell restaurant, had assaulted and raped the proprietress, and had then vanished with most of her cash. It was now confirmed that, although blind, the escaped detainee was equipped with a radarlike device that enabled him to see. He was described as being armed and dangerous.

Tallon smiled wryly. The bit about rape was particularly good, coming from Amanda. He fell asleep and managed to doze most of the day, only coming fully awake when low growls from Seymour announced that people were moving around outside. Nobody came into the shed, and after a while Tallon stopped thinking about what he would do if they did. Winfield's philosophy that a man had to do his best with the present and leave the future to itself was not especially attractive to Tallon, but it was the only one that worked in the present circumstances.

At dusk he gathered up Seymour and the pack and cautiously opened the door. As he was about to step out a large plum-colored limousine swept up the short driveway and rolled to a halt outside the main house. A thickly built young man got out, with his jacket slung over his arm, and waved to someone in the house who was beyond Tallon's field of vision. The young man walked toward the front entrance, stopped at a bed of pale blue song-flowers, and knelt down to remove a weed. At his touch the flowers began a sweet, sad humming that was clearly audible in the dark confines of the shed.

The song-flowers were a native variety that fed on insects, using the plaintive humming sound to attract or lull their prey. Tallon had never like them. He listened impassively for a moment, holding Seymour's eye to the narrow opening of the door. The heavy-set man discovered several more weeds and uprooted them; then, muttering furiously, he came toward the shed. Tallon slipped the automatic out of his pocket, reversed it in his hand, and stood waiting as the crunching footsteps reached the other side of the door.

This was exactly the sort of thing he had hoped to avoid. His training was such that he could beat most any man in physical combat; but having his eyes tucked under one arm was going to make a big difference.

He tensed himself as the door latch moved.

"Gilbert," a woman's voice called from the house. "Change your clothes if you're going to start gardening. You promised."

The man hesitated for two or three seconds before turning and moving away toward the house. As soon as the man was inside the house Tallon slipped out of the shed and hit the road again.

He kept it up for four days, traveling a short distance by night and hiding out during daylight, but the deterioration in the eyeset's performance was becoming more noticeable. By the end of the fourth night, the picture he was getting was so faint that he would almost have been better off with the sonar torch. His name had gradually faded from the newscasts, and so far he had not seen a single member of the E.L.S.P. or even of the civil police. He decided to begin traveling in daylight again.

Tallon walked for three more days, not daring to try hitching a ride. He now had plenty of money, but the risk of eating in restaurants or even at lunch counters seemed too great, so he lived on the bread and the protein preserves he'd taken from The Persian Cat, and by drinking water from the ornamental fountains along the way.

Seeing it from the point of view of a pedestrian, Tallon was aware, as never before, of Emm Luther's desperate need for land. The density of population was not particularly high, but it was completely uniform—the residential developments, interspersed with commercial and industrial centers went on without end, filling every square mile of level land the continent had to offer. Only where uplands merged into actual, hostile mountainsides did the waves of neat, prefabricated buildings fall back in defeat. Some attempt was made at agriculture in the high borderland areas, but the planet's real farming space was the ocean.

Tallon had covered almost one hundred miles before realizing that he was going to be able to see only poorly for perhaps two more days and would then be blind again—with 700 miles still to go.

The only faint ray of hope was that the Block would

know he was out of the Pavilion. All members of the network would be on the lookout for him, but the organization had never been strong on Emm Luther. New Wittenburg was the planet's only entrance point, and the E.L.S.P. automatically put tracers on every Earthsider who took up residence. It was quite possible that at that very moment good agents were being caught as they broke their covers in order to try to intercept Tallon. He decided to keep on the road for one more day and head for the railway again.

The next day passed without incident. Tallon was aware that none of the newscasts had given an adequate description of the eyeset, although Amanda must have been able to furnish one. He figured there was some kind of censorship at work, perhaps to avoid an official scandal over the fact that dangerous political prisoners had been given facilities to manufacture highly sophisticated artificial eyes. He sensed that Helen Juste might be in trouble; but the main thing, as far as Tallon was concerned, was that the general public had no idea what they were looking for. Anybody interested enough to look for someone using a "radarlike device" might reasonably expect to see a man with a black box and rotating antenna on his head. As it was, spectacles were a fairly common sight, never having been fully supplanted by contact lenses; and Tallon in his dusty, anonymous uniform blended into most backgrounds. His unremarkable appearance had been one of his major assets in the service of the Block.

The following day was slightly colder, and there was a little rain, the first Tallon had seen since his arrest. His route had never taken him far from the coastal railway system, and now he began walking toward the ocean again. The dullness of the day was magnified by the somber images produced in the failing eyeset, and Tallon hurried to make the most of the measured amount of light left to him. Late in the afternoon he caught a glimpse of the ocean, and shortly afterward saw the glint of railway tracks.

Slanting north again to where he guessed the next railway station to be, Tallon found himself approaching the first really big industrial development he had seen on his journey. Behind a high perimeter fence the sawtooth roofs of the factory receded into the gathering dusk for almost a mile before terminating in the banked glowing windows of a design and administration block. The roar of powerful air-conditioning machinery reached Tallon as he walked by the fence, puzzled at the contrast between this huge plant and the typical family business setup prevailing on Emm Luther. Several dark green trucks passed, slowing down to go through a lighted and patrolled entrance a hundred yards ahead, and Tallon glimpsed the book-and-star emblems that marked them as the property of the government.

Tallon now began to understand. The immense, noisy complex was one of the factors that had put him in his present situation. It was part of the chain of government factories that was draining the planet of its technological cream in a massive production program for interstellar probes.

Here were built parts for the fantastically expensive robot ships that were launched from Emm Luther at the rate of one every fifty-five seconds, year in, year out. More than half a million probes a year—as many as were produced by Earth itself—were triggered into open-ended jumps and the consequent lonely destinies of flicker-transits. The planet had bled itself white in the effort, but the gamble had paid off with a new world.

Now the factories were swinging over to the crash production of everything needed to make Aitch Mühlenberg a going concern before Earth found a foothold. The land area of the new world was still secret, but if Emm Luther could put in two settlers, with support material, for every square mile before any other power found its way there, then by interstellar law the whole planet would be hers. Ironically, the law had been promulgated mainly by Earth, but that had been in earlier days, when the mother world had not foreseen the emancipation of her children.

The police cruiser was moving slowly, almost sleepily, when it passed Tallon. There were two uniformed officers in front and two plainclothesmen in back. They were smoking cigarettes with a peaceful concentration, getting ready to go off duty, and Tallon could tell they were sorry they had seen him by the reluctant way in which the cruiser stopped. They even hesitated before they got out and began walking back to him—four small-town cops who could see their evening meals growing cold if this dusty stranger turned out to be the man they had been told to look for.

Tallon was sorry too. He looked down the long featureless road, then ducked his head and ran for the factory entrance. It was about twenty yards in front of him, so he had to run toward the police for a few seconds. They walked a little faster, glancing at each other, then gave startled shouts as Tallon cut through the entrance and loped across the tarmac apron leading to the nearest building. Hampered by the pack and the struggling dog, Tallon could only lumber along, and was surprised when he reached the lofty doors safely. Squeezing through the narrow opening, he looked back toward the gate and saw that the factory security men had belatedly come alert and were arguing with the police.

Inside the vast hangarlike room rows of storage racks held yellow plastic drums, hermetically sealed transit packages for electronic units. Tallon ran down an aisle, turned into one of the narrower transverse passages, and climbed into a rack, nestling down among the cylinders. As far as he could tell, there had been nobody in the room when he'd entered. He took out the automatic and cuddled the butt in his hand, suddenly conscious of how useless it was to a man with his particular handicap. It was doubtful if he would be able to persuade Seymour to look down the sights long enough to let him draw a decent bead on an elephant.

As the hammering in his heart eased off he reviewed his position. Nobody had come into the building yet, but that was probably because they were spreading out around it. The longer he waited, the less chance he'd have of getting out. Tallon dropped down from the rack and ran toward the end opposite to where he had come in. It was almost dark, but he could see that the walls of the building consisted of overlapping sliding-door systems throughout. Each of the huge doors had a standard-size door in it, which meant he could get out anywhere—provided he picked an exit that did not have someone waiting outside it.

Almost three-fourths of the way along the building he crossed to one of the small doors, hesitated a second, and slowly edged it open. There was a flat, vicious *crack*, and something hot plowed its way across his shoulders. Tallon leaped back from the door, which now had a circular, metal-tongued hole in it. Seymour was yelping loudly with fright and scrabbling at Tallon's ribs while outside the raucous cries of startled seabirds drowned the gun's echoes.

Wrong door, Tallon thought belatedly. He ran to the end of the building and grabbed a door handle, but did not pull it open. The unseen person who had fired at him would probably expect him to try again at the gable doors. He could now be waiting outside this very door. Tallon continued across the end of the building to another door, but he realized that his opponents would figure out that move as well. He could go back to the first door, but valuable seconds were racing by while he played guessing games; reinforcements were coming up, and everything was on their side. He couldn't even see to shoot at them because he had to use the eyes of——

Of course!

Tallon's fingers flickered over the eyeset's selector studs. At the fifth attempt he was outside, flying in the darkling air, while down below him the dimly seen figures of two men moved along the many-doored gable. His spiraling flight took him higher . . . a glimpse along one side . . . more figures running . . . a dizzy, sweeping descent . . . another side of the same building . . . small trucks parked close to the wall, but no men in sight . . .

Tallon reselected Seymour's eyes, oriented himself, and ran for the nearer wall. He burst out of a door, ran between two empty trucks, crossed a roadway, and went into a building like the one he had left. There were more lines of storage racks here, but this hangar was brightly lighted and stacker trucks were whining their way down several of the aisles. Tallon forced himself to walk slowly across the building. None of the truck drivers seemed to notice him, and he got to the other side and out into the cool evening air without any difficulty.

The next building was as deserted as the first. When he emerged from it Tallon judged that he was far enough from the center of activity to abandon cover. He went down the separating alley, moving away from the front boundary of the industrial complex. At the corner, the failing eyeset provided him with a misty view of scattered small buildings, stockyards, cranes, pylons, lights. To the northwest, the curving snouts of two furnaces reared up into the indigo sky. Factory whistles were hooting, great doors were slamming shut, cars with bright headlights were streaming toward the entrances.

Tallon realized he had been lucky to have the sprawling industrial nightmare close by when he had to run. He was aware of a warm stream of blood trickling down his back; and he realized that his legs were folding under him, and that he was on the verge of blindness.

The obvious thing to do now, Tallon thought, is to give myself up—except that I've given up giving myself up.

He angled off across the factory area, staggering a

little, leaning against walls when walking became too difficult. Tallon knew he would present a ludicrous picture to anyone who looked at him, but two things were in his favor: in big state-owned projects the employees tend to see only what concerns their own work, and at the end of a shift they see even less.

An hour or two went by; then he found himself in the vicinity of the giant furnace stacks. Aware that he would have to lie down very soon, he picked his way across treacherously sliding piles of fuel and reached the rear of the furnaces, seeking a place of warmth. The fence marking the rear perimeter of the area loomed up above a jungle of climbing weeds. Tallon guessed he was about as far as he could get from the searching policemen and security guards, and he looked for a place to rest.

Between the furnaces and the fence, the climbing weeds and grasses were growing over untidy scrap heaps of packing cases and rusting metal framework, which looked like discarded assembly jigs. The big fires were quiescent in their ceramic ovens, but the heat from the stacks warmed the whole area. Tallon investigated several of the vegetation-shrouded heaps before he found a hole big enough to hide in. He slid wearily into the dusty little hole and pulled a screen of grass back over the entrance.

Maneuvering around for comfort, he discovered he could stretch out full length in the confined space. He gingerly put out his hand and found there was a tunnel leading toward the center of the stack, roofed and walled with random chunks of steel and discarded packing materials. Tallon wriggled a little farther in, then the effort became too great. He struggled free of the pack, laid his head on it, switched off the eyeset, and allowed the whole stinking universe to tilt away from him.

"Brother," a voice said in the crawling darkness, "you have not introduced yourself."

There were four of them—Ike, Lefty, Phil, and Denver.

The big attraction, Ike explained, was the heat. In every human society there are a few who are not equipped to make the grade, who have neither the will to work nor the strength to take. And so they live on scraps that fall from rich men's tables. You will always find some of them in those few places where one or more of life's necessities can be obtained simply by putting out a hand and waiting. Here there were falling scraps of heat that on a long

84

winter's night could mean the difference between sleeping and dying.

"You mean," Tallon said drowsily, "that you're hoboes."

"That's putting it crudely," Ike replied in his thin nasal voice. "Have you any more of that delicious stale bread? Nature's toast, I call it."

"I don't know." Tallon's back was hurting now and he longed for sleep. "How could I tell in the dark, anyway?"

Ike's voice was mystified. "But, brother, we have our lumi-lamp on. Can't you look in your bag? We're hungry. Your new friends are hungry."

"Sorry, new friend. I'm too tired to look, and if I wasn't too tired it wouldn't make any difference, because—" Tallon made the effort—"I'm blind." It was the first time he had ever announced it to anyone.

"I'm sorry." Ike really sounded sorry. There was a long silence; then he said, "Can I ask you a question, brother?"

"What is it?"

"Those heavy gray glasses you're wearing—why have blind men started wearing heavy gray glasses? What good are they when you have no eyes?"

Tallon lifted his head a few inches. "What do you mean?"

"I mean, what's the point of wearing———"

"No!" Tallon broke in. "What did you mean when you said blind men have started wearing heavy gray glasses?"

"Well, brother, yours is the second pair I've seen this week. Ten miles or so north of here is a private estate owned by a very rich man who's blind. Denver and I often climb the wall, because we both like fruit. The fruit trees there are overloaded, and it seems a shame not to relieve them of their burden. There are the dogs, of course, but during the day———"

"The glasses," Tallon interrupted. "What about the glasses?"

"That's it, brother. We saw the blind man this week. He was walking in the orchards and was wearing glasses like yours. Now that I think of it, he was walking like a man who can see!"

Tallon felt a surge of excitement. "What's his name?"

"I forget," Ike replied. "I know he's supposed to be related to the Moderator himself, and that he's a mathematician or something. But I don't remember his name."

"His name," Denver said eagerly, "is Carl Juste."

85

"Why do you ask, brother?" Ike sniggered. "Did you think he might be a friend of yours?"

"Not exactly," Tallon said coolly. "I'm more a friend of the family."

thirteen

Ike's price for acting as a guide was one hundred hours.

The figure shocked Tallon somewhat. In his two years on Emm Luther he had grown used to the radical "fiscal democracy" the government had imposed soon after it came to power in 2168. The original and purest form ordered that for every hour a man worked, regardless of his occupation, he would be paid a monetary unit called "one hour." These were divided, like the Lutheran clock, into one hundred minutes; the smallest unit was the quarter—one-fourth of a minute, or twenty-five seconds.

When the uprising that had resulted in the ending of Earth's mandate had died down, the Temporal Moderator had found it necessary to modify the system considerably. Complex factorization clauses had been added, allowing those who effectively increased their contribution to the economy by self-improvement to be paid more than one hour per hour. But the absolute top was a factor of three, which was why there were few large private corporations on Emm Luther—the incentive was limited, as the Moderator intended it to be.

To approach factor three, a man had to have the highest professional qualifications and use them in his job—yet here was a shiftless hobo named Ike demanding what Tallon conservatively estimated as factor ten.

"You know that's immoral," Tallon said, wondering if he had that much money. He had forgotten to count the roll of bills he had stolen from The Persian Cat.

"Not as immoral as it would have been had I taken the money while you were sleeping and disappeared with it."

"Obviously you've checked that I have the money. As a matter of interest, how much is in my pack?"

Ike tried to sound embarrassed. "I made it about ninety hours."

"Then how could I pay you a hundred?"

"Well—there's the radio."

Tallon laughed sharply. He supposed he was lucky at

that. He was blind, and the wound across his shoulders stiffened his body with agony every time he moved. The four tramps could have rolled him during the night; in fact it was surprising they were prepared to do anything at all in return for his money.

"Why are you willing to help me? Do you know who I am?"

"All I really know about you, brother, is what I can tell from your accent," Ike said. "You're from Earth, and so are we. This was a good world till that bunch of Bible-waving hypocrites took it over and made it impossible for a man to get an honest day's wage for an honest day's work."

"What was your work?"

"I had no work, brother. Health reasons. But it's just as well, isn't it? If I had been working I wouldn't have got paid for it in good honest solars, would I? Denver here used to sell pieces of the True Cross. . . ."

"Till they closed down his production plant, I suppose," Tallon said impatiently. "When can you get me to the Juste estate?"

"Well, we'll have to hole up here for the rest of the day. We'll get you through the fence after dark. After that it's just a matter of walking. We can't stroll along the boulevards, of course, but we'll be there before dawn."

Before dawn, Tallon thought; or, if he was unable to get his eyeset back from Carl Juste, before the final nightfall. He wondered if the man who had it was Helen Juste's father or brother.

"All right," he said. "You can take the money."

"Thank you, brother. I already have."

At Tallon's request, Ike allowed him to make the overnight walk with the eyeset switched off to save his last glimmer of sight for whatever he would have to face when he reached the estate. Only Ike and Denver went with him, and each took one of his arms.

As his two companions guided him through a weed-hidden break in the perimeter fence and out to where the quiet avenues began again, Tallon wondered how their breed had survived the centuries without change. The continuous development of civilization seemed not to have touched them; they lived and died in a manner no different from that of vagrants in ancient times. If the human race went on for another million years, perhaps at the end of that time there would still be men like these.

"By the way," Tallon asked, "what will you do with all that money?"

"Buy food, of course." Ike sounded surprised.

"And when it's finished? What then?"

"I'll live."

"Without working," Tallon said. "Wouldn't it be easier to take a job?"

"Of course it would be easier to take a job, brother, but I'm not going to go against my principles."

"Principles!" Tallon laughed.

"Yes, principles. It's bad enough not getting paid in good honest solars, but the crazy system makes it worse."

"How? It seems like a reasonable idea to me."

"I'm surprised at you, brother. Factorization itself is a good idea, but they apply it backward."

"Backward?" Tallon wasn't sure if Ike was expressing an honest opinion or making a devious joke.

"That's what I said." Ike wasn't kidding. "It happens on Earth, too. Take somebody like a surgeon. That man *wants* to be a surgeon—he wouldn't do any other job in the world—and yet he gets paid ten or twenty times as much as some poor guy who is doing work he hates. It isn't right that somebody like—what do you call the head man on Earth right now?"

"Caldwell Dubois," Tallon supplied.

"Well, he likes being head man, so why should he get so much more money than somebody who has to mind a machine he hates the sight of? No, brother, there should be a kind of psychological checkup every year on everybody who's working. When it shows that somebody is starting to like his job, his pay should be cut, and that would provide extra money for another guy who hates his work a bit more than he did the year before."

"I'll pass your thoughts on to Caldwell Dubois the next time I see him."

"We've got a real celebrity here," Denver said. "After he's had sherry with the Justes he's going on to dinner with the president of Earth."

"Talking about your principles," Tallon said to Ike, "would they allow you to give me back a little money for train fare?"

"Sorry, brother. Principles is principles, but money is money."

"I thought so."

Tallon walked on blindly, allowing himself to be shoved unceremoniously into gardens or doorways every time an automobile went by. The two men accepted without question his need to avoid being seen, and they got him to the

Juste estate without incident. Tallon wondered if, in spite of what Ike had said, they really did know who he was. It would explain their willingness to help him in this way and also their readiness to take advantage of him.

"Here we are, brother," Ike said. "This is the main gate. It will be daylight in less than an hour, so don't try going in there in the dark. The dogs are unfriendly."

"Thanks for the warning, Ike."

Tallon released his grip on the bars of the massive steel gate and dropped to the ground. In the gray half-light he saw himself through the eyes of Seymour, who had already wriggled through the bars and waited patiently while Tallon went over the top. The eyeset, completely unused for a day and a half, was giving a faint picture at maximum gain. It had reached the stage at which its useful life could be measured in minutes.

"Come on, boy," Tallon whispered urgently. Seymour leaped up into his arms, spinning Tallon's universe around him, but he had become used to the occasional disorientation that was bound to occur when his eyes had four legs, a tail, and the mind of a terrier. Although he had never been interested in animals as pets, Tallon had developed a strong affection for Seymour.

With the dog tucked under his arm and the automatic pistol in his hand, Tallon walked cautiously up a gravel driveway that wound through tumbled banks of dense shrubbery. He lost sight of the gate immediately, and found himself moving thrugh a tunnel of overhanging trees and lush dark foliage. The drive wound back on itself twice before coming to a misty park. There were many trees here too, but Tallon was now able to see a low rambling house on top of a small hill, with a series of ascending terraces.

It was then he heard the dogs howling their deep-throated indignation at his presence in the grounds. The awful sound was followed by a fierce crackling of foliage as they came racing to find him. To Tallon they sounded as big as horses, and although he had not seen them yet, they seemed to be moving at top speed.

He spun round once on his heels, equivalent to turning the head in a normally sighted person. There was nothing to be gained by running back into the bushes, and the house was at least four hundred yards away and uphill. Some of the trees growing on the terraces had trunks that separated into three or four thick curving branches just above the round. Tallon ran to the nearest one and scrambled into the narrow cleft.

The dogs—three gray shapes—appeared off to his left, skimming along the edge of the shrubbery. They looked like a local hairless mutation of original wolfhound stock, with huge flat heads carried close to the ground. Their howling grew louder as they saw Tallon.

He began to raise the automatic, but Seymour's body convulsed in Tallon's arms at the sight of the large bounding dogs. Before Tallon could adjust his grip the little dog was down on the grass, yelping with fear and scuttling frantically back toward the entrance gates. Tallon shouted desperately as he saw, at one side of Seymour's vision, one of the gray shapes separate from the others to intercept the terrier. Then Tallon had to think about his own situation, for without the use of Seymour's eyes he was, literally, easy meat.

His fingers flicked the eyeset controls, reselecting on proximity, and he got behind the eyes of the nearest dog. It was a little like watching a film shot from the nose of a low-flying jet—a tremendous sense of arrowing flight, ground flowing rapidly underneath, stands of tall grass looming up, like hills, and being effortlessly penetrated as though they were green clouds. Up ahead, apparently rocking slightly because of the barreling motion, was a human figure, with a white desperate face, hanging onto the curving arms of a tree.

Tallon forced himself to raise the automatic and move his arm around until, from the viewpoint of the speeding animal, the weapon's muzzle was a perfect black circle, with equal foreshortening of the barrel. The trick, he thought grimly, is to try to hit myself right between the eyes. He squeezed the trigger and was gratified to feel an unexpectedly powerful kick from the automatic. But, apart from one slight shudder, the shot made no difference to the rapidly expanding image he was receiving from the hound.

He tried again. This time the sound of the shot was followed by a deep bark of pain and surprise. He got images of crazily rotating sky and ground, then a close-up of grassy roots, which swiftly darkened into night. Mentally reeling from the shock of his own vicarious death, Tallon reselected for the next dog. He saw himself in the same tree, but much closer this time—*and from the back.*

Twisting awkwardly in the confined space of the tree trunks, Tallon fired instinctively and was rewarded by instantaneous blindness. That meant he had made a perfect kill. Wondering at the effectiveness of the little weapon, he ran his fingers over the machined metal and discovered that the muzzle, instead of being a simple circle, was a cluster of six tiny openings. Amanda Weisner apparently took no chances when she chose a weapon. The automatic was the kind that fired six ultra high-velocity slugs at a time, one from the center and five from slightly divergent barrels. At close range the small gold-plated automatic would obliterate a man; at longer distances it was a pocket-sized riot gun.

Not hearing any movement close by, Tallon pressed the number one stud—Seymour's—and got only blackness. With a pang of grief, he tried the eyeset on "search and hold," and picked up the third dog. It was moving through the heavy shrubbery quite slowly, and there was redness over the blurred area of snout obtruding in the lower edge of the picture.

Angry now, and with confidence in his armament, Tallon got out of the tree. Moving with noisy carelessness, he picked up his fallen pack and went up the hill in the direction of the house. As he had left the eyeset tuned in on the remaining dog, he was blind as far as his own movements were concerned, and he kept his arms outstretched in case he hit any trees. He could have fished the sonar torch out of the pack, but he was not expecting to get far before seeing himself through the third dog's eyes. His guess was correct. The dog burst through the close-packed bushes, and Tallon got a dim picture of his own figure trudging toward the house. Once again the ground began to flow underneath in great flying bounds.

He waited until his back filled the picture before he turned, with the flaming automatic jarring his wrist, and put out the lights. That's for you, Seymour, he thought. For services rendered.

Tallon turned his attention to the problem of getting into the house without Seymour's aid. Ike had told him Carl Juste lived alone in his semimansion, so he was not worried about having to deal with more than one person; but he could not see and the untended wound had turned his shoulders into a rigid area of pain. Besides, the noise made by the gun and the dogs could have alerted Juste. It occurred to Tallon that if Juste was making use of the other eyeset he must have one or more animals of some sort near him.

Tallon put the eyeset back on "search and hold," but got no picture. He then got out the sonar torch and, with its help, hurried toward the house. Only four or five minutes had elapsed since he climbed the steel gates. As he neared the house he began to get dark, fleeting images; the only recognizable feature was a near-bright oblong area that was a window viewed from inside the house.

He was unable to decide if it was really that dark inside, or if the eyeset was on the point of final failure. Closer still, with his feet on what seemed to be a paved patio, he made out other details. He was looking at a lavishly furnished bedroom, apparently from a point quite high on one of the walls. As he was trying to figure out what sort of creature would provide such an unusual view, another area of the room became relatively clear.

A powerfully built bearded man was sitting up in the bed with his head tilted in the attitude of someone straining to hear. He seemed to be wearing heavy spectacles.

The high-pitched scream of the sonar told Tallon he had almost walked into a wall. He swung left and went along the wall, hand over hand, looking for a door. In the bedroom the man stood up and took something like a pistol from a drawer. Tallon's hands found the recess of a window. He swung his pack at it but the tough glass bounced it back at him. Stepping back a few paces, he raised the automatic and blasted the glass out of its frame.

While he was scrambling blindly into the room, his view of the bedroom shifted abruptly, and in a characteristic manner with which Tallon had become familiar. The seeing creature was a bird, possibly a falcon, which had just flown to its master's shoulder. Tallon saw the bedroom door grow large in his dim vision, and knew Juste was coming to find the intruder. He ran recklessly across the room he was in, wondering how he was going to fare in the weird battle about to take place. Both men were seeing through the same third pair of eyes, so each would see exactly what the other saw. But Juste had two advantages: He had almost no disorientation, because his eyes were perched on his own shoulder; and his eyeset was in good condition.

Tallon considered the possibility of avoiding any kind of a fight. Perhaps if he told Juste who he was and why he was here, they would be able to work something out. He found a door in the room's inner wall and turned the knob. The picture he was getting as he did so was a view from a landing looking downstairs into a spacious hall

93

with doors on each side, which meant Juste had come out of his bedroom and was waiting for Tallon's next move.

Tallon eased the door open and saw a dark crack appear at the edge of one of the doors in the hall. As always, he experienced a strange dismay at the feeling of being in two places at once.

"Juste," he shouted through the opening, "let's not be stupid. I'm Sam Tallon—the guy who invented that thing you're wearing. I want to talk to you."

There was a long silence before Juste answered. "Tallon? What are you doing here?"

"I can explain that. Are we going to talk?"

"All right. Come out of the room."

Tallon began to open the door wider, then saw he was looking at the dark crack along the barrel of a heavy, blued-steel pistol.

"I thought we agreed not to be stupid, Juste," he shouted. "I'm wearing an eyeset too. I'm tuned in on your bird, and I'm looking right down the sights of that gun you have in your hand." Tallon had just become aware of his one slight advantage—the man who had the eyes with him was bound to transmit tactical intelligence to the opposition.

"Very well, Tallon. I'm setting my pistol on the floor and stepping away from it. You can see that, I presume. You leave yours on the floor in there and come out, and we'll talk."

"All right." Tallon set the automatic down and went out into the hall. In the dimness of the picture from his eyeset he saw himself emerge from the doorway. He felt uneasy, not because he suspected Juste would cheat, but because he knew he himself would probably have to cheat to get what he wanted. Halfway to the foot of the stairs he halted, wondering how he could ever separate Juste from the eyeset without violence.

Juste must have given some kind of signal to the bird, but Tallon missed it. Only because he was already familiar with the swooping sensations of bird flight saved Tallon from being numbed by dislocation when the attack came. As his own image ballooned up he dived for the door; he had reached it when the clawing fury descended on his shoulders. Hunching to protect his jugular, Tallon fought through the door, feeling razors slicing cloth and skin. He slammed the door hard, catching the bird between its edge and the jamb, and drove his weight against it. There was a harsh scream, and it was black again.

He discovered one claw was hooked right through the

94

tendons in the back of his left hand. Working in blindness, he took the knife out of the pack and hacked the claw free from the bird. It was still buried in his hand, but that would have to wait. He scanned with the eyeset, got no picture, picked up his automatic, and opened the door again.

"Dark, isn't it, Juste?" His voice was hoarse as he shouted into the hall. "You should keep more than one bird in the house. We'll dispense with our talk. I'm going to take those eyes back from you and be on my way."

"Don't try to come near me, Tallon." Juste fired two deafening shots in the confines of the hall, but neither of the slugs came near Tallon.

"Don't waste your ammunition. You can't see me, but I can get to you, Juste. I have something Helen didn't take, and it doesn't need eyes."

The pistol roared again, and was followed by the sound of tinkling glass. Guided by the electrical tones of the sonar, Tallon ran for the foot of the stairs and stumbled up them. He reached Juste about halfway up, and they came down hard, fighting. Tallon, sick with fear for the remaining good eyeset, wasted no time on his bigger, stronger, though untrained, opponent. Initiating the rhythms of the Block-developed pressure-feedback combat system, Tallon held nothing back; and before they had reached the floor Juste was a dead weight.

Tallon, who had been cradling the big man's head during the last part of the fall, took off Juste's eyeset and exchanged it for his own. All that remained now was to find some more money and food, then get out in a hurry.

Wishing there were some way to test the eyeset for possible damage, he put it on "search and hold" and was amazed when he got a picture. Sharp, strong, and beautifully clear.

A close-up of a heavy polished entrance door swinging open, and beyond it, the frozen tableau of himself crouched over the sprawling form of Carl Juste. Tallon was able to see the shocked expression on his own hunted, blood-streaked face.

"You!" a woman cried out, "what have you done to my brother?"

fourteen

"Your brother's all right," Tallon said. "He fell down the stairs. We were arguing."

"Arguing! I heard the shots as I drove up to the house. I'll report this immediately." Helen Juste's voice was cold and crackling with anger.

Tallon raised the automatic. "Sorry. Come in and close the door behind you."

"You realize how serious this is?"

"I haven't been laughing much." Tallon stood back while she closed the door and went to her brother. He wished he could look at Helen Juste, but as she had the only functioning eyes in the house, he saw nothing except her neatly manicured hands moving over Carl Juste's unconscious face. As before, in her presence he was aware of powerful stirrings deep within him. Her hand came away from the back of Juste's head, with traces of blood in the lines of the palm.

"My brother needs medical attention."

"I've told you he's all right. He'll sleep for a while. You can tape up that cut if you want." Tallon spoke confidently, knowing he had given Juste's nervous system enough abuse to keep him under for perhaps an hour.

"I want to do that," she said; and Tallon noticed the complete absence of fear in her voice. "I have a first-aid kit in my car."

"In your car?"

"Yes. I'm not likely to drive off and leave my brother alone with you."

"Get it then." Tallon had an uneasy feeling he was losing the initiative. He walked to the door with her and waited while she went to her car and took the kit from a compartment. The car was a sleek luxury job with gravity negator skids in place of wheels, which was why he had not heard it arrive. He watched her hands at work with the gauze pads and tape, and he almost envied Carl Juste for a moment. Tallon's head ached, his shoulders were on fire, and he was way beyond ordinary tiredness. Lying

96

down to sleep when you are tired, he thought, was a pleasure more exquisite than eating when you were hungry, or drinking when you were thirsty. . . .

"Why did you do this, Detainee Tallon? You must have realized my brother is blind." She spoke almost abstractedly as she worked.

"Why did *you* do it? We could have made three eyesets, six, a dozen. Why did you allow the Doc and me to have them when you were planning to take them away from us?"

"I was prepared to stretch the law for the sake of my brilliant brother, not for the sake of convicted enemies of the government," she said stiffly. "Besides, you still haven't explained this senseless attack."

"My eyeset got damaged, so I had to take this one." Tallon felt a wave of irritation, and his voice rose. "As for the senseless attack, if you look around you'll find a few bullet holes in the walls. And none of them were made by me."

"Nevertheless, my brother is a harmless recluse, and you are a trained killer."

"Listen, you," Tallon shouted, wondering what the conversation was really all about, "I have a brain too, and I'm not a——" He broke off as he discovered her eyes had left her brother and were giving him a steady picture of his own left hand.

"What's wrong with your hand?" She sounded, at last, like a woman.

Tallon had forgotten the embedded claw. "Your harmless brother had a harmless feathered friend. That's part of its undercarriage."

"He promised me," she whispered. "He promised me not to——"

"Louder, please."

There was a silence before she answered, speaking normally again. "It's hideous. I'll remove it for you."

"I'd be grateful." Suddenly weak, Tallon stood by while she covered her brother with a blanket. They went through a door at the rear of the hall and into a chrome and white kitchen that bore traces of untidy bachelor living. Helen Juste was carrying the first-aid kit. He sat at the cluttered table and allowed her to work on his hand. The touch of her fingers seemed only slightly more substantial than the recurrent warmth of her breath on the torn skin. He resisted the temptation to bask in the welcome feeling of being cared for. New Wittenburg was a long way to the north, and this woman was a new obstacle to his getting there.

"Tell me," she said, "is Detainee Winfield really . . . ?"

"Dead," Tallon supplied. "Yes. The rifles got him."

"I'm sorry."

"For a convicted enemy of the Lutheran government. You surprise me."

"Don't try that approach with me, Detainee Tallon. I know what you did to Mr. Cherkassky when you were arrested."

Tallon snorted. "Do you know what he did to me?"

"The injury to your eyes was an accident."

"Damn my eyes. Did you know he put a brain-brush on me and tried to wipe my life away like you just did to the stains on this table?"

"Mr. Cherkassky is a senior Lutheran executive. He wouldn't."

"Forget it," Tallon said brusquely. "That's what I've done. Whatever it was—I've forgotten it."

When she had finished with his hand and taped the wound he flexed the fingers experimentally. "Will I ever play again, Doctor?"

There was no reply, and he felt a creeping sense of unreality. Helen Juste eluded him; he was unable to imagine her as a human individual, to visualize her place in this world's society. Physically he could see her only fleetingly when she happened to glance at her own reflection in the kitchen mirror. He noticed, too, that she kept glancing toward a shelf on which lay several small pieces of soft leather, stitched into the shape of bags. Their purpose mystified him; then he remembered Juste's bird and that it had been trained for falconry.

"How ill is your brother, Miss Juste?"

"What do you mean?"

"How did he react to the eyeset? Did he like hunting with his birds? Running with the dogs?"

She went to the window and stared out at distant trees, limned against the red disk of the rising sun, before answering. "It isn't your business."

"I think it is," he said. "I didn't realize what was happening at the time. I knew Cherkassky was coming. There was no time to wait for the answer to the problem of the cameras, so I decided to look through the eyes of other men. It was that simple. I had no idea I was creating the first new form of perversion the empire has seen in a long, long time."

"You mean, you . . . ?"

"No, not me. I've been running too hard. But there was that woman in Sweetwell—the one I'm supposed to have raped. She used the eyeset when I was sleeping. She liked cats, if you know what I mean."

"What makes you think Carl was like that?"

"*You* do, though I don't know why. Something about the way you keep insisting he's a harmless recluse, perhaps. There may not be any sex angle in his case, of course. I've read that when a person who has been blind for a long time has his sight restored, it isn't always the expected joyful experience. There can be depression, feelings of inadequacy caused by suddenly being back on even terms with the rest of humanity, with no handicap to fall back on. How much better to be, say, a falcon, with sharp eyes and sharper claws and a mind that doesn't understand weakness, or anything but hunting and tearing and——"

"*Stop it!*" . .

"I'm sorry." Tallon was faintly surprised at himself, but he had wanted to reach her and felt he had succeeded to some extent. "Do you treat only those wounds your brother has inflicted? There's this hole in my back. . . ."

Helen Juste helped him to work the uniform down from his shoulders, and gasped when she saw the great pool of congealed blood that lay across his back. Tallon almost gasped too as he received the picture. He had never before really appreciated the degree of nastiness that can be covered by the phrase "nasty flesh wound." This was nasty, it was fleshy, and it was a wound in anybody's book.

"Can you do anything with it—short of amputating my shoulders, that is?"

"I think so. There wouldn't be enough tissue welder and bandages in my own first-aid kit, but Carl usually has some in this cupboard." She opened it, found the medical supplies, and got to work on his shoulder with a moistened cloth, gently removing the superfluous mess. "This is a gunshot wound?"

"Yes." Tallon told her how it had happened. He had almost convinced himself she was a sympathetic listener when he suddenly thought of something. "If you knew your brother had medical supplies in here," he said slowly, "why did you go out to the car for your own kit?"

"No reason. Force of habit. You know, you should be in bed with an injury like this. Why don't you give yourself up and get proper attention before the reaction sets in?"

"Sorry. I'm going to have something to eat now; then

99

I'll tie you up, along with your brother, and be on my way."

"You won't get far."

"Perhaps not. Does it matter much to you, anyway? I had an idea you and the Pavilion might be parting company after this little affair. Is that why you're here now? Have you been sacked?"

"Detainee Tallon," she said evenly, "escaped prisoners do not interrogate prison executives. I'll make breakfast now. I'm hungry too."

Tallon was mildly pleased at her reaction. He got into his uniform again, then took the roll of medical tape and bound Carl Juste's wrists and ankles. The big man smelt of brandy. Tallon returned to the kitchen and sat in a chair, feeling the tingle of the tissue welder compound on his back, while Helen Juste cooked something that was so like ham and eggs he was almost certain it was ham and eggs. Twice, as they were eating, Carl Juste moaned and stirred slightly. Tallon allowed Helen Juste to go out and look at her brother each time.

"I told you he'd be all right," he said. "He's a big, strong boy."

He made no further attempts to talk to her during the meal, but enjoyed the faint echo of domesticity he received from the act of eating breakfast with a young woman in the morning quietness of a warm kitchen, even though they were much more than worlds apart.

Tallon was sipping his fourth cup of strong coffee when he heard a scratching sound at the entrance door at the far end of the hall. The scratching was followed by a shrill bark Tallon recognized.

"*Seymour!*" he shouted. "Come in, you little phony. I thought you were dead."

He went to the door ahead of Helen Juste and was almost embarrassed at the joy he felt on seeing the familiar brown shape leap into his arms. As far as he could tell from where Helen was standing, the dog was unharmed. Perhaps Seymour had made it to the gate and got through the bars inches ahead of the big hound. If the latter had inefficient brakes, it could explain the redness he had detected around its muzzle; and it was also possible that Seymour had been rocketing along fast enough to be out of range when Tallon had tried to pick him up on the eyeset.

Hugging the excited animal to his chest, Tallon reselected on proximity, and put Seymour on his number one stud again. Equipped once more with what were practically his own eyes, he turned to look at Helen Juste. She was as perfect as he remembered, still wearing the green Pavilion uniform, which accented her coloring. Her hair was a massive copper helmet, burnished laser bright; her eyes, still the color of whiskey, were looking past him, at her pale blue car.

Tallon had a strong hunch about that car. He went over to it and opened the door. A small orange light was winking patiently, low on the dash—on the radio panel, to be exact. The TRANSMIT toggle was in the "on" position, and the microphone was missing from its clip.

Breathing heavily, Tallon switched the radio off and went back into the house. Helen Juste was staring at him, white-faced but very erect.

"Full marks for resourcefulness, Miss Juste," he said. "Where's the microphone?"

She took it from her pocket and held it out to him. As he expected, it was the type that incorporated a miniature transmitter of its own in place of a wire connection to the main radio. He had been on the air for some time, no doubt on a police wavelength. Tallon had almost forgotten the automatic pistol in his right hand. He raised it thoughtfully.

"Go ahead and shoot me," she said calmly.

"If you had thought I would shoot, you wouldn't have taken the risk," Tallon snapped, "so spare me the bit where you face the mouth of the cannon without flinching. Get your coat, if you have one here. We haven't much time."

"My coat?"

"Yes. I don't trust myself driving your car. Seymour has an unfortunate habit of not looking where I want him to look, and at high speed that could be dangerous. Besides, it will do no harm to have you as a hostage."

She shook her head. "I'm not leaving this house."

Tallon reversed the pistol, weighed it meaningfully in his hand, and took one step forward. "You want to bet?"

As they were going out the door Carl Juste seemed to come fully awake. He gave several moans, each time a little louder, until he was almost shouting; then as his mind took over he abruptly fell silent.

"I don't want to leave him like that," Helen Juste said.

"He'll have company pretty soon. Remember? Just keep moving."

Tallon turned and looked back at Carl. He was strug-

101

gling ineffectually with his bonds; his forehead glistened with sweat, and the blind eyes shuttled frantically. Tallon hesitated. He knew only too well how the big man was feeling after his long uphill climb from unconsciousness into a private black hell of sightlessness, helplessness, and hopelessness.

"Just a minute," he said. He went back and knelt beside Carl Juste. "Listen to me, Juste. I've taken the eyeset back because I need it more than you do. Can you hear me?"

"I hear. . . . But you won't . . ."

Tallon raised his voice. "I'm leaving you another identical eyeset, which needs only a new power unit to make it work again. I'm also writing out a full specification of the power unit for you. If you don't let the police or agency men take it as material evidence, you should be able to get the eyeset working again soon. With your sort of money, it should be no problem to bend the relevant laws."

He signaled to Helen Juste, and she ran for paper and pen. Tallon seized them and, still kneeling on the floor, began writing the specification. While he worked, Helen mopped her brother's forehead and spoke quietly to him in a sad small voice that Tallon scarcely recognized. There was something deep and strange about their relationship. He finished writing and crammed the paper into the pocket of Juste's pajamas.

"You wasted a lot of time," Helen Juste said as he stood up. "I didn't expect such . . ."

"Stupidity is the word. Don't remind me. Now let's move."

The car was smooth, quiet, and fast. As Tallon had noted earlier, it was an expensive imported job of advanced design, with a gravity component engine that instead of propelling the vehicle allowed it to *fall* forward. Spaceships used similar power units in the initial stages of flight, but because of the difficulty of fitting them into a confined space they were rarely used anywhere else, even on aircraft. This meant the car was very expensive indeed. Helen Juste handled it with showy skill, broadsiding through the gate she had left open on her arrival, and taking off along the roadway with a prolonged burst of acceleration that sucked Tallon deep into his seat.

As the car swooped around a long curve, which blended into a motorway, Tallon held Seymour up to look through the rear window. Seymour was a little nearsighted, but there seemed to be specks in the southern sky, moving with the characteristic sinking flight of helicopters.

"Switch on the radio," Tallon said. "I want to hear what crimes I've committed this time."

They listened to music for half an hour; then the program was interrupted for a newsflash.

Tallon whistled. "That was quick. Now let's hear how depraved I've become since my last public appearance." But as the announcer spoke, Tallon felt embarrassed at his display of egotism; his name was not mentioned.

The official news was that Caldwell Dubois, for Earth, and the Temporal Moderator, for Emm Luther, had simultaneously recalled their diplomatic representatives following the breakdown of the Akkab negotiations over apportionment of new territories.

Unofficially, the two worlds were on the verge of war.

fifteen

Helen Juste: Twenty-eight years old, unmarried, beautiful, honors degree in social sciences at the Lutheran University, member of the planet's premier family, holder of a governmental executive position—and a complete failure as a human being.

As she drove northward she tried to analyze the interactions of character and circumstance that had led to her present situation. There was her older brother, of course, but perhaps it was too easy to blame everything on Carl. He had always been there, looming big, a kind of landmark by which to steer through life; but over the years the landmark had crumbled.

The erosion began when their parents and Peter, their younger brother, were drowned in a speedboat accident near Easthead. Carl, in his last year at university, was driving the boat. He began to drink heavily after that, which would have been serious enough on any other world. On Emm Luther, where abstention was part of the very political and social structure, it was almost suicidal. He managed to hold together for three years, joining the space-probe design center as a mathematician; then a case of substandard bootleg brandy had cost him his eyesight.

She helped install him in his private estate, which would have cost a prohibitive amount had the Moderator not fixed it for Carl, partly out of family feeling and partly out of a desire to get him tucked safely away from the public eye. Since then, she had watched Carl grow more and more neurotic, break up into smaller and smaller pieces.

At first she had assumed she would be able to help; but looking within herself, she had found nothing to offer Carl. Nothing to offer anybody. Just a tremendous sense of inadequacy and loneliness. She tried to get Carl to emigrate temporarily with her to another world, perhaps even to Earth itself, where an operation to give him some form of artificial vision would have been legal. But he had been afraid to go against the Moderator's wishes, to face the soul-attenuation of the flicker-transits, to leave the comfortable womb-darkness of his new home.

When Detainee Winfield had told her about Tallon's idea for a seeing device it had seemed to be the answer to everything, although, looking back, she realized she had been wrong to suppose that making Carl happy in that particular way would have compensated for her personal inadequacies. She had broken every rule in the book to bring about the creation of the seeing devices, finally going too far for even the Moderator's protection, only to see Carl use his new eyes to seek out other forms of darkness. . . .

After Winfield and Tallon had made their preposterous escape there had been a preliminary investigation by the prison board; as a result, she had been suspended from duty and confined to her quarters pending a full inquiry. An impulse had led her to slip away and head north to see Carl for perhaps the last time, and—with a strange inevitability—Tallon had been there too.

She glanced at Tallon, sitting beside her in the front seat, with the dog lying sleepily across his knees. He had changed since the first day she saw him walking so hesitantly with the box of the sonar torch strapped to his forehead. His face was much thinner, taut with strain and fatigue, but somehow more composed. She noticed that his hands, resting lightly on the dog's tousled back, were at peace.

"Tell me," she said, "do you really believe you'll get back to Earth?"

"I don't think that far ahead any more."

"But you're anxious to get back. What is Earth like?"

Tallon smiled faintly. "The kids ride red tricycles."

Helen stared at the road. It was beginning to rain, and white road markers streamed under the car like tracer bullets aimed from the darkening horizon ahead.

Some time later she noticed that Tallon had begun to shiver. Within minutes his face was covered with perspiration.

"I told you to give yourself up," she said casually. "You need attention."

"How long will it take to reach New Wittenburg if we don't stop?"

"Assuming you want me to keep within the speed limit—about ten or eleven hours."

"That's heading straight north? Along the strip?"

"Yes."

Tallon shook his head. "Cherkassky is probably waiting for me along the strip, and he's bound to have a description of this car. You'd better head east, up into the mountains."

"But that will take a lot longer, and you haven't even the strength to hold out till we reach New Wittenburg the short way." Helen wondered vaguely why she was arguing over the welfare of the unimpressive Earthsider. Can this, she thought with a sense of shock, be the way it begins?

"Then it doesn't matter which way we go," Tallon said impatiently. "Head east."

Helen took the first lateral road they came to. The car hummed effortlessly through several miles of neatly laid out, high-density residential developments, identical to all the others on the continent. Suburbia without the *urbs*. She wondered again what her life would have been like had she been born on another planet, into an ordinary family. Without the social isolation of rank, she might have married and had children ... to someone—the thought came unbidden, yet with the force of a planet in its orbit—like Tallon. She sheered away from it. In another life she could have traveled; he had done that too, more than anybody she had ever met before.

She glanced across at Tallon again. "Is space flight very frightening?"

He started slightly, and she realized he had been drifting into sleep.

"Not really. They give you equanimol shots an hour before the first jump, and a whiff of something stronger before the ship hits the portal. The next thing you know, you've arrived."

"But have you ever done it without tranquillizers and anaesthetic?"

"I've never done it *with* them," Tallon said with unexpected force. "You know the one big flaw in the null-space drive, as we employ it? It's the only form of travel ever devised that doesn't broaden the mind. People shunt their bodies right across the galaxy, but mentally they're still inside the orbit of Mars. If they were made to sweat it out without shots, to feel themselves being spread thinner and thinner, to know what flicker-transits really mean— then things might be different."

"What sort of things?"

"Like you being a Lutheran and me being an Earther."

"How strange," she said aloud; "an idealistic spy." But she made a silent acknowledgment to herself: This *is* the way it begins. Twenty-eight years it had taken her to

106

discover that she could not become a complete human being by herself. The sad thing was that it had begun with someone like Tallon and would therefore have to be stopped right away. She saw that his eyes were closed again behind the heavy frames of the eyeset, and that Seymour had slipped into a contented doze—which meant Tallon was in darkness and drifting into sleep.

She began to draw up a plan. Tallon was weakened by strain, exhaustion, and the effects of his wound, but something about his long thoughtful face told her he would still be too much for her to handle alone. If she could further lull him and keep him awake till nightfall, it might then be possible to do something after he'd gone to sleep. She searched for a subject that would interest him, but could think of nothing. The car was moving into the green foothills of the continental spine when Tallon himself began to talk in an effort to fight off unconsciousness.

"Something puzzles me about the Lutheran salary system," he said. "Everybody gets paid in hours and minutes; and even with the factorization clauses, the maximum that, say, a top-notch surgeon could earn in an hour is three hours—right?"

"Correct." Helen repeated familiar words: "In his wisdom, the first Temporal Moderator removed the temptations of unlimited material gain from the path of our spiritual progress."

"Never mind the catechism. What I want to know is, how can somebody like your brother, and presumably the rest of your family, have so much more money than anybody else? How does that estate of Carl's, for instance, square with the system?"

"It squares with the system, as you put it, because the Moderator accepts no payment at all for his services on behalf of the people of Emm Luther. His needs are taken care of by voluntary donations from his flock. Anything he receives in excess of his needs is disposed of as he sees fit, usually to relieve suffering or need."

"The head man shares his bounty with his friends and relatives," Tallon said. "I wish Doc Winfield were here."

"I don't understand."

"Who does? What field of mathematics was your brother in?"

Helen was about to make a sarcastically evasive answer suitable for a political agent who poked his nose into the realm of higher mathematics; then she remembered Tallon's work on the seeing devices. And an entry in his dossier, she now recalled, stated that he had begun his career as a researcher in domain physics before, inexplicably, becoming a kind of supertramp and finally an agent.

"I couldn't understand Carl's work," she said. "It had something to do with the theory that the null-space universe is much smaller than ours—perhaps only a few hundred yards in diameter. He told me once that the two-light-second spheres we call portals might correspond to single atoms in the null-space continuum."

"I've heard the idea kicked around," Tallon replied. "Was he getting anywhere with it?"

"You know that all information about space-probe design is grade-one classified."

"I know; but you said you couldn't understand it anyway, so what can you give away?"

"Well . . . as far as I know, Carl was on the team that decided the jump increment and coordinates for the Aitch Mühlenberg probe. The round trip has a smaller number of portals than any other route in the empire. Carl said it meant they could build cheaper spaceships, though I don't see why."

"Ships for the Aitch Mühlenberg run would be cheaper because they wouldn't need such high reliability standards in their positional control equipment. With a smaller number of hops, there's less chance of something going wrong along the way. But that probe was an isolated success, wasn't it? They weren't able to pick up any other worlds using the same sort of math."

"I suppose not," Helen said, concentrating on the ascending sweeps of the road, "but Carl didn't believe it was pure coincidence."

"I know how he felt. It's tough to give up a perfectly good theory just because it doesn't fit the facts. Is he doing anything with it now?"

"He's blind now."

"So what?" Tallon spoke harshly. "A man doesn't have to lie down just because he loses his eyes. Of course it took someone like Lorin Cherkassky to teach me that, so perhaps I have an advantage over your brother."

"Mr. Cherkassky," Helen said impatiently, "is a senior executive of the Lutheran government and——"

"I know; if there were flies on Emm Luther he wouldn't harm one of them. The government of Earth has its faults, but when there's a dirty job to be done, it does the dirty job. It doesn't subcontract the work to somebody else and pretend nothing's happening. I'll tell you something; I'll tell you what Mr. Cherkassky is really like."

Helen did not interrupt as Tallon told her about his

arrest, the use of the brain-brush, his attack on Cherkassky, the blinding, and his certain knowledge that Cherkassky would finish him off at the first opportunity.

Helen Juste let Tallon talk because it kept him awake, which meant he'd sleep more soundly later; and somewhere along the way she understood that everything he was saying was true. Unfortunately it made no difference: He was still an enemy of her world, and his capture was still her passport back to her former position of trust and responsibility.

She drove more slowly now. Tallon kept on talking, and she found it easy to join in. By the time dusk had begun to drift down from the sky in minute gray specks, they had gone beyond mere conversation into real communication—an experience completely new to Helen. She had risked calling him Sam, working it in as naturally as possible, and he had accepted the implied shift in their relationship without comment. He seemed to have grown smaller, as if his illness had caused him to physically shrink; mentally he was suffering from fatigue. Aware of his condition, Helen now made her move.

"There's a motel up ahead, Sam, and you've got to sleep."

"And what would you be doing while I slept?"

"I'm calling a truce. I've been a long time without sleep, too."

"A truce, sweetie—why?"

"I told you—I'm tired. Besides, you took a risk to help Carl; and after what you told me about Mr. Cherkassky, I don't want to be the one to hand you over to him." It was all true, and she found it was easy to lie when you were telling the truth.

Tallon nodded thoughtfully, eyes closed, sweat gleaming on his forehead.

The motel was on the outskirts of a small community that was gathered on a ledge of the mountain range. Along the central part of the main street, store windows shone in the evening twilight and tubes of colored neon were bright threads against the towering black mass of the peaks beyond. The town was quiet, even at that early hour, as it huddled at the bottom of an invisible stream of cool wind that coursed from the uplands toward the ocean.

Helen stopped the car at the motel office and paid for a double chalet. The manager was a leaden-eyed, middle-aged man in an unbuttoned shirt—the archetype of all motel managers—who took her money mechanically, seeming hardly to hear her story that her husband was suffering from a cold and had to rest as soon as possible. She took the key and drove the car along the row of vine-covered chalets to number 9.

Tallon was holding the automatic in his right hand when she opened the car door at his side, but he was shivering so violently she was almost tempted to disarm him herself. There was no need, however, to take even that much of a chance. She helped him out of the car and into the chalet, supporting almost half his weight. He kept muttering apologies and thanks to nobody in particular, and she knew he was close to delirium. The rooms were cold and smelled like snow. She steered him onto the bed, and he curled up gratefully, like a child, as she pulled the covers over him.

"Sam," she whispered, "there's a drugstore a couple of blocks away. I'm going to get something for you. I won't be long."

"That's right. . . . You get me something."

Helen stood up with the automatic in her hand. She had won, and it had been easy. He spoke as she was going out the bedroom door. "Helen," he said weakly, using her name for the first time, "ask the police to bring me a few extra blankets when they come."

She closed the door quickly and ran through the little living room out into the sharp night air. What did it matter that he knew where she was going? Her mind kept straying into an endless mirror-dialogue—I know; I know you know; I know you know I know. . . .

The truth of the matter, she decided, was simply that she felt guilty about handing him over, knowing what she now knew about Cherkassky, knowing what she now knew about Tallon. He was too ill to do anything about it, but it had been important to her to trick Tallon in exactly the same way she would have tricked him had he been well. All right. He had seen through the trick. She could stand a little more guilt.

Helen opened the car door and got in. Seymour uncurled from the passenger seat and nuzzled her hand. Pushing the dog away from her, she reached for the radio panel, then pulled back her hand. Her heart had begun a slow, steady pounding that stirred the hair at her temples. She got out of the car and went back into the chalet, locking the door behind her.

As she stood over the bed, removing the eyeset from his face, Sam Tallon moved restlessly and moaned in his sleep.

This, she thought as she unbuttoned the blouse of her uniform, is the way it all begins.

sixteen

A spring morning, lovely with pastel mists, had moved in over New Wittenburg, bringing a feeling of life to the tree-lined streets, laying bars of clear, fresh sunlight across the concrete desert of the space terminal.

"This is as far as we go," Tallon said as the car topped a rise in the road and he saw the city spread out before him. "I can walk from here."

"Must we split up?" Helen slid the car over to the side of the road and allowed it to sink onto the ground. "I'm sure I could help you."

"This is the way it has to be, Helen. We've been over the whole thing already." Tallon spoke firmly to cover his own feelings of dismay at leaving her. The five days they had spent together at the motel had passed like so many seconds. In terms of affecting his life, however, they might have been decades. In loving her he had found both youth and a new level of maturity. But now the pea-sized capsule buried in his brain had acquired even greater importance than the brand-new planet it represented. Two other worlds were at stake, for if it came to war, neither Earth nor Emm Luther would survive in its present form.

It had taken him some time to persuade Helen that they ought to split up on reaching New Wittenburg. She had been unimpressed when he'd pointed out that slipping away from the Pavilion in defiance of an order was one thing, being caught in his company was another. In the end, he had told her he would be unable to make contact with his own agents while in the company of a government prison official.

"You'll call me at my hotel, won't you, Sam?"

"I'll call you." Tallon kissed her once, briefly, and got out of the car. As he was closing the door she caught his sleeve.

"You *will* call, Sam. You won't leave without me?"

"I won't leave without you," Tallon lied.

With Seymour tucked under his arm, he began to walk into the city. The pale blue car ghosted past, and he tried

111

for a last glimpse of Helen, but Seymour jerked his head in the wrong direction. He had deemed it necessary for them to separate because if he and Cherkassky should meet again, it would be here in New Wittenburg. The trouble was, no matter how things worked out, the separation was going to be permanent. If he were to get off the planet undetected, there would be no coming back; and with what his escape would cost Emm Luther, there would be no hope of Helen's being free to follow him.

Tallon walked quickly, staying relaxed, but keeping an eye out for patrol cars or uniformed men on foot. He had no definite plan for making contact, but New Wittenburg was the one city in which the Block had been able to build an effective organization on Emm Luther. His original orders had been to stay on the loose near the space terminal until he was contacted, and that was what he intended to do now, three months later. Considering the publicity his escape from the Pavilion had received, the organization was bound to be making preparations to receive him.

The contact came sooner than he expected.

Tallon was moving along a quiet street, heading in the general direction of the hotel where it had all started, when he suddenly lost vision. He stopped and fought down the surge of panic, then discovered that moving his eyes slightly to the left brought back his sight. Evidently the signal beam from the eyeset had been deflected from the optic nerve juncture, which suggested he had entered a powerful force field of some sort. He had just decided it must be emanating from the interior of a heavy truck parked beside him at the curb when—*snap!*

Tallon staggered and grabbed for support. He was in a long narrow box, lined with power circuitry and lighted by a single fluorescent tube overhead. Hands caught him from behind, steadying him.

"That was neat," Tallon said. "I guess I'm inside the truck."

"Correct," a voice said. "Welcome to New Wittenburg, Sam."

Tallon turned and saw a tall, youngish, thin-shouldered man, with tousled hair and a slightly crumpled nose. They both lurched as the truck began to move.

"I'm Vic Fordyce," he said. "I was beginning to think you'd never get here."

"So was I. Why didn't somebody go south to watch for me along the way?"

"They did. And most of them were in the Pavilion

112

before your bunk had a chance to cool down. The E.L.S.P. boys must have staked out every Earthsider on the planet. One suspicious move and that was it."

"I thought it might be like that," Tallon said. "Cherkassky is thorough, if nothing else. But what was the idea of grabbing me off the sidewalk? Wouldn't it have been easier to open the door and whistle?"

Fordyce grinned. "That's what I said; but this rig was specially built to lift you right out of an E.L.S.P. cruiser, if necessary, and I guess they didn't want to let all that perfectly good grav-component gear go to waste. Talking about special gear—are those glasses the radarlike device we've been hearing about? How in hell did you get the chance to build something like that?"

Tallon thought of Helen Juste and it hurt. "It's a long story, Vic. What happens next?"

"Well, I have a drug pack here in the truck. I'm to administer it while the boys up front cruise around the city; then we take you to the spaceport. You should be on board your ship within an hour."

"Within an hour! But the schedule——"

"Schedule!" Fordyce interrupted excitely. "Sam, you're an important man now; scheduled flights are out as far as you're concerned. The Block has sent a special ship for you. It's registered on Parane as a merchantman, and you're going aboard as a crew replacement."

"Won't look a bit suspicious? What if some spaceport official starts checking on why a Paranian ship should come to Emm Luther just to pick up a new crewman?"

"That would take time, and once you're aboard the *Lyle Star* you're as good as home. It looks like a merchantman, but it's fast and has the firepower of several battle cruisers. They're prepared to flatten the whole city to get you out."

Fordyce moved about the gently swaying interior of the truck, switching off the grav-component equipment. Tallon sat down on a box and stroked Seymour, who lay on Tallon's knees and uttered low growls of contentment. After what he had been through, Tallon thought, it was impossible to believe he was almost in the clear. Within an hour, a mere hundred minutes, he would be on board a ship and ready to lift off from New Wittenburg, leaving behind him Lorin Cherkassky, the Pavilion, the swamp, Amanda Weisner—everything connected with this world. And Helen. The thought of leaving her was especially painful now that the final break was imminent.

Fordyce unfolded a low stretcherlike cot along the floor

and opened a black plastic box. He motioned to the bed.

"There it is, Sam. Lie down on this and we'll get on with the job. I'm told this hurts a bit, but it wears off after a few hours."

Tallon lay down and Fordyce stooped over him.

"In a way you're lucky," Fordyce said as he held a syringe up to the light. "The masking of the eye pigmentation and retinal patterns is always the most painful, but you've nothing to worry about, have you?"

"You sound like the medic back in the Pavilion," Tallon replied wryly. "He seemed to enjoy *his* work, too."

The treatment was not as bad as Tallon had anticipated. Some of the processes—darkening his skin and lightening his hair—were completely painless; others hurt a bit, or were uncomfortable. Fordyce worked quickly and expertly as he administered the necessary injections. Some of the needles were inserted just beneath skin of Tallon's fingertips, distorting the patterns. Some were plunged deep into major muscle groups, producing tension or relaxation, subtly altering his posture, his bodily dimensions, even his walk. The same techniques, on a reduced scale, were applied to his face.

While the drugs were taking effect Fordyce helped Tallon change into fresh clothing from the skin out. The suit was gray, casual, and completely nondescript, which looked right for a spacehand laying up between tours of duty. Tallon enjoyed the civilized feel of clean clothing against his skin, especially the shoes and socks, although the shoes were built up to make him appear taller.

"That's it, Sam," Fordyce said finally, with evident satisfaction. "You wouldn't know your own mother, or something like that. Here are your papers and your new identity. They're more than good enough to get you through the spaceport checkpoints."

"How about money?"

"You won't need it. We're dropping you right at the terminal. You'll have to get rid of the dog, of course."

"Seymour stays with me."

"But what if——"

"Was there any mention of a dog being with me—from official sources, or in any of the papers or broadcasts?"

"No, but——"

"Then Seymour stays." Tallon explained that his eyeset worked by picking up optic nerve signals from the dog's eyes. And besides, he liked Seymour and would have been taking him anyway. Fordyce shrugged and looked carefully unconcerned. The truck began to slow down, and Tallon picked up the dog.

"Here we are, Sam," Fordyce said. "The space terminal. When you get through the main gates take the slideway to the north side. You'll find the *Lyle Star* in docking area N. 128. Captain Tweedie will be expecting you."

Suddenly Tallon was reluctant to go. Space was big, cold, and endless, and he was not prepared for it.

"Listen, Vic," he stalled, "this is a bit sudden, isn't it? I was expecting to talk to someone here in New Wittenburg. Doesn't the cell leader want to see me?"

"We're processing you just the way the Block wants it done. Goodbye, Sam."

The truck began to move as soon as Tallon had stepped down. He lifted Seymour to his chest and surveyed the half-mile stretch of passenger and cargo entrances, from which branches of slideways and roads fanned out toward a dazzling white concrete horizon. Vehicles of all shapes and sizes moved among the reception buildings, warehouses, and vast service hangars. The gleaming whalebacks of ships in their cradles sparkled in the morning sun; and high up in the blue of the sky were the bright sequins that were other ships drifting in on finals.

Tallon took a deep breath and began to walk. He discovered that the treatment not only changed his appearance; it also made him feel different. He walked steadily, but with a strange rhythm, noting that buses and taxis were discharging their passengers outside the gates and onto the main slideway system. Joining the steady stream of pedestrians, he found the entrance reserved for port officials and flight crews. The bored-looking clerk barely glanced at his papers before handing them back. Tallon noticed two other men lounging in the office behind the clerk. They too seemed totally uninterested in flight personnel; but Tallon had no doubt that sensors, linked to a computer, had scanned and measured him from head to foot, and would have screamed their plastic heads off had he fit their specifications.

Hardly believing he was through the checkpoint so easily, Tallon took the north-bound slideway, looking for the *Lyle Star* as the high-speed belt carried him between rows of ships. It was a long time since he had been so close to space vessels, and through Seymour's eyes he saw them with a new clarity, suddenly aware of how unreal they looked in the morning light. The huge metal ellipsoids lay helplessly in their cradles, many of them with raised hatches that were cantilevered like insect's wing casings.

115

Cargo-handling and servicing vehicles were clustered at the open hatches.

There were no other exploitable worlds in the Lutheran system, so all the ships in the port were interstellar craft, fitted with three entirely separate drives. Gravity negators were used at take off, allowing the big ships to fall upward into the sky; but these were effective only so long as there was a strong gravitic field available to be twisted back on itself. When a planet's portal was a long distance off, as most of them were, ion-reaction drives punched the ships out to it in the old-fashioned way. Then came the null-space drives that—in some half-understood way—sucked the big ships into another universe in which the game of energy versus mass was played with different rules.

Tallon noted that of the many uniforms he saw in and around the terminal, the gray cords of the E.L.S.P. men were the most common. There was no doubt that the net was out for him, yet he had strolled right through it. Although Cherkassky's resources were limited compared with those of the Block, this was, after all, his home ground. It was almost as if . . .

A sign reading "N.128" loomed up, and Tallon edged across the progressively slower strips until he could step off onto the concrete. He began walking down a lateral row of ships, looking for the centaur symbol carried by Paranian vessels. A few paces along the row a slab-shoul-dered giant, in a black uniform with gold insignia, stepped out from behind a crane, in whose shade he had been standing.

"You're Tallon?"

"That's right." Tallon was taken aback by the stranger's size. Everybody looked big to Tallon while he was carry-ing his eyes under his arm, but this man was extraordinary, a towering pyramid of muscle and bone.

"Captain Tweedie of the *Lyle Star*. I'm glad you made it, Tallon."

"I'm glad, too. Where's the ship?" Tallon tried hard to sound glad, but he kept thinking about the eighty thousand portals that lay between Emm Luther and Earth. Soon they would be between Helen and himself. She would be waiting in a hotel room in New Wittenburg, and he would be eighty thousand portals away, so many giant zigzag steps across the heavens, with no chance of getting back. Red hair and whiskey-colored eyes. . . . No colors in the dark. . . . *I wish I were where Helen lies*. . . . No colors, but texture and warmth and communion. . . . *Night and day on me she cries*. . . .

116

Tweedie pointed toward the far end of the line and began to walk quickly. Tallon kept up with him for several yards, then realized it was no good this way.

"Captain," he said calmly. "You go on ahead to the ship and wait for me."

"What do you mean?" Tweedie turned instantly, like a huge cat. His eyes flashed from beneath the visor of his cap.

"I've got to go back into the city for an hour; I left something behind." Tallon kept his voice flat and cool while his mind kept chanting, *What am I doing? What am I doing? What . . .*

Tweedie smiled humorlessly, showing unusually thick teeth. "Tallon," he said with exaggerated patience, "I don't know what you're thinking about, and I don't want to find out. All I know is, you will board my ship—*right now.*"

"I will board your ship," Tallon said, taking a step back, "in an hour from now. Since when did chauffeurs start giving orders?"

"This is a new category of treachery, Tallon. You'll not survive it."

"What do you intend doing about it, Captain?"

Tweedie shifted his feet and leaned his bulk forward slightly, like a wrestler preparing to bomb a smaller opponent. "Let's put it like this," he said stiffly. "The Block is interested in getting your head back to Earth. Whether it's still attached to your body, or not attached to your body, is a minor detail."

"You'll have a job catching me," Tallon said, backing away, "unless you want to call a policeman. There are plenty of them about at the moment."

Tweedie crooked his massive fingers, the joints making audible cracks, then glanced around him helplessly. A pair of E.L.S.P. men were drifting past on the slideway only a few paces from him, and his ship was a good four hundred yards away across the crowded apron.

"Sorry, Captain." Tallon walked confidently toward the moving belt. "You'll have to be patient a little longer. You can have your most comfortable G-cell ready for me when I get back."

"I warn you, Tallon." Tweedie's voice was thick with anger and frustration. "If you get on that slideway, you'll make the trip back to Earth in a hatbox."

Tallon shrugged elaborately and kept walking. Ten minutes later he was back on the roadway outside the airport entrance. Getting out had been even easier than getting in. He stuffed his papers into an inside pocket, then shifted the uncomplaining Seymour to a more comfortable position on his chest while he decided the best way to reach Helen's hotel. Off to his right a commotion broke out at one of the entrances, and he automatically turned in the opposite direction.

It would take some time to reach Helen, and he would have to be more careful than ever. Tweedie had not been joking. Sam Tallon had crossed up the Block—something a man did only once—and now two groups of agents would be fanning out through the city, looking for him. Knowing the Block as he did, Tallon was uncomfortably aware that his chance for survival would probably be better if the E.L.S.P. got to him first.

Hunching his shoulders to light a cigarette, Tallon walked into the city.

seventeen

Tallon was surprised to discover he had one advantage over his adversaries. The discovery came when he glimpsed his own reflection in a store window and failed, for a moment, to recognize himself. What he saw was a tallish, fair-haired stranger walking with a round-shouldered professorial gait. His face seemed broader, composed of flatter planes, and Tallon knew himself only by the dog tucked under his arm.

That, he decided, would also be a useful identification for Earth agents as well. He thought about it for a moment, then had an idea. The chance was worth taking.

"Down you go, Seymour," Tallon whispered. "You've been a passenger far too long."

He set the dog at his feet and commanded him to heel. Seymour yelped and sped round Tallon's ankles several times in frantic, skidding turns. Steadying himself in a suddenly whirling universe, Tallon gave the order to heel again and was relieved when the dog, apparently having expressed his feelings to his own satisfaction, obediently fell in behind him.

He began to walk again, guided by Seymour's affectionate view of his rising and falling heels, but it proved too difficult, and he adjusted the eyeset controls until he received vision from someone behind him. Helen was staying at the Conan on South 53rd Street, a hotel she had frequented on previous visits to the city. It was some four miles from the spaceport.

Periodically cursing his lack of taxi fare, he plodded on through the unseasonable heat, feeling the built-up shoes beginning to blister his heels. He saw patrol cars nosing through the traffic several times, but they were obviously on routine circuits of the city. Once again Tallon found himself thinking vaguely that it was all too easy, that his luck was too good to be true.

The Conan turned out to be, by Emm Luther standards, a first-class hotel. Tallon halted in a doorway on

119

the opposite side of the street and considered a new problem. Helen Juste was probably a minor celebrity—as a relative of the Temporal Moderator, a member of the prison board, and a woman of some wealth—and therefore an easy mark for the police, especially while staying at a hotel in which she was known. Walking up to the desk and asking for her could be the last mistake he would get the chance to make.

He decided to wait where he was and watch for her either leaving or entering the hotel. Half an hour went by and it seemed an eternity; Tallon began to feel he should move on. Then he had another thought: How did he know Helen was in there at all? She could have been taken away already, or unable to get a room, or she could have changed her mind. He dithered for another ten minutes, until Seymour began to get restless and started tugging on his trouser leg. Tallon got an idea; the dog seemed to be intelligent, so why not . . . ?

"Listen, boy," Tallon whispered, hunkering down beside Seymour. "Find Helen. In there. *Find Helen.*" He pointed to the hotel entrance, where several groups were standing and talking.

Through the eyes of a passerby Tallon saw Seymour scramble across the street and disappear, with wagging tail, into the lobby. He reselected Seymour's vision signals and immediately was weaving an uncertain course throug⋅ the lobby, only a few inches above the carpet. There were more close-ups of stairs, skirting boards, and door jambs. Tallon, fascinated by the dog's progress, could almost hear him sniffing as he tried for Helen's scent. Finally he was looking at the base of a white door, saw forefeet paw at it, and then Helen's face appeared, curious, surprised, laughing.

When she carried Seymour out to the street Tallon glimpsed his own gray-clad figure waiting in the doorway across the street. He waved, and she crossed the street and came over to him.

"Sam! What's happened to you? You look——"

"There's no time, Helen. Do you still want to try flicker-transits?"

"You know I do. What do I need to pack?"

"There's no time for packing either." Having got this far, Tallon suddenly felt sick with anxiety, with the feeling that his luck couldn't hold out. "If you've got cab fare we'll leave right now."

"All right, Sam. I've got the cab fare."

With Seymour under his arm, Tallon took Helen's hand,

and they started walking and looking for a cruising taxi. He explained most of the situation to her as they walked. A few minutes later they caught a vacant robo-cab. Tallon fell back in the seat while Helen punched out their destination and fed a bill into the waiting rollers. His nerves were twanging a thin fierce tune, like high-tension cables in a gale. He wanted to scream. Even touching Helen and looking at her made no difference; the whole universe was falling in on him, and he would have to run very, very fast. . . .

In the last block before the space terminal, Tallon reached out and pressed the button that stopped the cab. They got out and walked the rest of the way, Tallon's instincts making him feel safer on the ground.

"When we get to the entrance," he said, "we'll have to separate for a few minutes. I'm supposed to be a Paranian crewman, so I go in by the staff entrance on the right. You get a sightseer's ticket and go in at one of the other doors. We'll meet at this end of the main north-bound slideway."

"Will it be all right, Sam? Surely nobody can simply walk onto a ship, without formalities, and fly away."

"Don't worry. Terminals like this are too big for centralized customs and emigration checks. There's a field neutralizer in every docking cradle that prevents the ship in it from lifting off until the customs and migration teams have worked it over."

"Isn't that just as bad from our point of view?"

"This is no ordinary ship. It'll have something on board to jam the neutralizer. We won't have to wait for any checks."

"But your people won't be expecting you to bring me aboard."

"Trust me, Helen. Everything's going to be fine." Tallon stretched his lips into a smile. He hoped it looked better than it felt.

Approaching the black tunnel of the crew entrance, Tallon felt icy sweat break out on his forehead. When Seymour's eyes had adjusted to the dim light of the tunnel Tallon discovered that nothing had changed. The same bored-looking clerk glanced perfunctorily at his papers; the same plainclothes men lounged in the cramped office. Tallon picked up his papers, walked on through to the sunlit edge of the field, and saw Helen waiting. She looked impossibly perfect, smiling as though they were going to a dance, Tallon thought, and had instinctive feeling that she was not a good dancer.

Tallon's gloom increased, though he could not pinpoint its cause. Then as they stepped onto the slideway the idea that had been prowling the hinterlands of his subconscious rose to the surface.

"Helen," he said, "how far is it from here to the Pavilion?"

"Something like a thousand miles—a bit more; I'm not certain."

"A long way for a blind man to travel without being picked up, especially when somebody like Cherkassky is on his tail."

"Well, you said you had been lucky."

"That's what's worrying me—I was never lucky before. I get the feeling that Cherkassky might be playing games. Picking me up on the road wouldn't be much of a feather in his cap; but suppose he let me get to where I was going first? Then he could net himself an Earth ship and its crew."

Helen looked subdued. "He'd be taking a big responsibility on himself."

"Perhaps not. The negotiations on Akkab over territorial acquisitions have broken down, but a lot of people in the empire think the Lutherians are holding on too tight, acting like dogs in a manger. It would suit Emm Luther quite well if a fat, juicy incident occurred—for example, a Block-owned ship disguised as a Paranian merchantman being caught in the act of smuggling out a spy."

The breeze began to flick Helen's hair as they moved over onto the higher speed strips of the slideway. She held the coppery strands in place with spread fingers.

"What are you going to do, Sam? Go back?"

Tallon shook his head. "I've quit going back. And, besides, I could be overestimating Cherkassky. This might be entirely my own idea and not his. It's funny, though, that I was able to walk into the city and to your hotel without any bother from either side. Lucky again, it seems."

"It seems."

"We'll get off this thing a little early, just in case."

They stepped off the slideway at N.125, three rows short of the one in which he had encountered Tweedie. Tallon noticed that Helen was still wearing her green uniform and did not look at all out of place in the anonymous activity of the field. Everything—from the ships themselves to the cargo-handling plant and cargo pallets—was on such a huge scale that two extra specks of humanity were all but invisible. It took them twenty minutes to reach the end of the row and start moving northward again. Tallon stopped when he saw the green centaur of Parane on the prow of a fat, silver-gray vessel up ahead.

"Can you read the name on that ship? Seymour's a little near-sighted."

Helen shaded her eyes from the lowering sun. *"Lyle Star."*

"That's the one."

He caught her arm, drew her into the lee of a line of cargo pallets stacked high with crates, and they began walking again, keeping out of the line of sight of anyone who might be watching from the ship. As he got closer Tallon saw that none of the cradles adjacent to the *Lyle Star* were occupied. It could be coincidence—or it could be that somebody had cleared a space for action. The ship itself was completely sealed up into flight configuration, except for the crew entrance door lying open near the nose. There was no sign of life on or near the vessel.

"It doesn't look right," Tallon said, "and it doesn't look wrong. I think we ought to hide somewhere and watch things for a while."

They moved closer, crossing open spaces only when lumbering mobile cranes provided cover, and got to within about a hundred yards of the *Lyle Star*. The light was fading, and the day crews were beginning to thin out to the point where the presence of two unauthorized persons might seem suspicious. Tallon looked around for a hiding place and decided on a crane parked close by. He brought Helen over to the massive yellow machine, which towered over their heads.. Opening an inspection hatch in the engine compartment, Tallon brought out his papers and stood glancing from them to the open hatch and back again, hoping he looked like a maintenance inspector at work.

"Make sure nobody's watching you," he ordered, "then get inside."

Helen gave a gasp of surprise and did as she was told. Tallon checked his surroundings, got in after her, and closed the hatch. In the choking, oil-smelling darkness they edged their way round the great rotary engines to the side of the crane nearest the *Lyle Star*. A row of ventilation louvers gave them a good view of the ship and the intervening area of concrete.

"I'm sorry about this bit of nonsense," Tallon said. "I suppose you feel like a kid hiding in a hollow bush?"

"Something like that," she whispered, and moved closer

123

to him in the blackness. "Do you often do this sort of thing?"

"It isn't usually this ludicrous, but the job does get pretty childish sometimes. As far as I can see, nearly all so-called affairs of state require at least one unfortunate to crawl along a sewer on his belly, or the like."

"Why don't you quit?"

"I intend to. That's why I don't want to risk walking into Cherkassky's arms at this stage of the game."

"But you don't really think he's in that ship?"

Tallon held Seymour to the nearest louver to see out. "No; it's just a possibility. But things look too quiet over there."

"Can't you tune your eyeset to someone inside and see who's there?"

"Good idea, but it doesn't work; I've just tried it. The signals are highly directional, and the hull must be too thick to let them through anywhere but at the direct vision panels—and they're all right up at the top of the nose section."

"How long do we wait in here then?" Helen had begun to sound depressed.

"Just till it gets a little darker; then we'll try Seymour. If he'll go in through the airlock, I should be able to keep in touch with him long enough to see if there's a reception party inside."

When the sun had gone down and the blue lights blazed on the perimeter of the field Tallon eased the little dog down onto the concrete, out through the ground-clearance space, and pointed him toward the ship. Seymour wagged his tail uncertainly and trotted toward the dark hull of the *Lyle Star*. Using Helen's eyes for a moment, Tallon watched the dog wander across the apron and up the short ramp. At the top, Seymour was silhouetted for a moment against the lemon-colored rays pouring from the ship's interior. Tallon pushed Seymour's stud on the eyeset just in time to get a dog's eye view of a booted foot lashing toward him.

Tallon, crouched in the crane's engine compartment a hundred yards away, heard Seymour's startled yelp. A few moments later the dog had returned to the crane and was shivering in Tallon's arms. Tallon soothed the terrier as he wondered what the next move should be.

It had been only a fraction of a second, but it was all he'd needed to recognize the blond, chunky sergeant who had assisted Cherkassky with the brain-brush the night they'd tried to erase Tallon's mind.

eighteen

Some time before dawn Tallon began to get persistent cramps in his legs. He worked furiously at the knotted muscles, wondering if the drug was wearing off or if it was a natural effect of the cold.

"What's the matter, darling?" Helen's voice was sleepy.

"My legs are killing me. Forty is far too old for perching all night on a cold engine block. What time is it?"

"My watch is back in the hotel. It must be near morning, though; I can hear birds."

"Birds are fine, but if you hear any people moving about in the cabin above us, get ready to move out." He put his arm around Helen's shoulders. She felt small and cold, and suddenly he was sorry for her. "Perhaps we should move out, anyway. Nobody's going to leave the ship."

"But if you go back into the city you'll be picked up sooner or later. Your only chance of getting back to Earth is here at the terminal."

"Some chance."

There was a long silence before Helen replied, and when she did her voice was crisp and cool—just as it had been when he first heard her in the Pavilion. "They'd come out if I told them where you were, Sam. I could go in to the ship and say you were hiding out in another part of the field."

"Forget it."

"But listen, Sam. I could say I had just got away from you while you were asleep, and you were getting ready to jump some other ship."

"I said forget it. Cherkassky, or whoever's in there, would hear the plot mechanism creaking. Stories like that never work, not on a professional, anyway. When you tell a lie, you've got to make it so outrageous that everybody will believe it, because you wouldn't say a thing like that unless it were true; or, better still, tell the truth, but do it in such a way that——" Tallon stopped abruptly as he got an icy blast of insight into the meaning of his own words.

"Helen, did they tell you in the Pavilion why I was arrested in the first place?"

"Yes. You'd found out how to get to Aitch Mühlenberg."

"What would you say if you were told I still had that information?"

"I'd say it was a lie. All that was erased, and you were checked and rechecked."

"You'd be underestimating Earth, Helen. The colonies forget how good we can be at some things. It's bound to happen, I guess. When you start off from scratch on a new planet, there's bound to be a shift in priorities—one type of frontier is extended, another is drawn back."

"What are you getting round to telling me, Sam?"

Tallon told her about the capsule that had snapped shut on a fragment of his brain, protecting it from all psychical and physical erasures, preserving in its submolecular circuits the information wanted by the Block. He felt Helen go rigid as he spoke.

"So that's why your people are taking so much trouble to get you back," she said finally. "I didn't realize I was helping you to hand a whole planet over to Earth. This makes a difference."

"You bet it makes a difference," he said. "Don't you know there's going to be a war over that planet? If I get safely out of here that war won't take place."

"Of course it won't take place; Earth will have what she wants."

"I'm not thinking in terms of governments," Tallon said urgently. "All that matters is the people, the civilians, the kids on red tricycles, who won't have to die if I get back to the Block."

"We all feel that way, but the fact remains that——"

"I could have gotten away," Tallon interrupted quietly. "I was at the ship and I turned back."

"Don't sound so tragic; it doesn't work with me. We've already decided that the security police planned to let you lead them to the ship. Even if it had got off the ground, there would have been interceptors of some kind between here and the portal."

"All right. So I would probably be dead. There would have been no megadeaths on my conscience."

"Your nobility routine is even worse than mine was."

"I'm sorry," Tallon said stiffly. "My sense of humor seems to have atrophied in the past few months."

126

Helen laughed delightedly. "Now you're actually being pompous." She leaned against him and kissed his cheek impulsively. Her face felt cold against his. "I'm sorry, Sam. You're right, of course. What do you want me to do?"

Tallon explained his idea.

An hour later, in the pewter light of dawn, Tallon checked the ammunition in the automatic and stretched his legs in preparation for running.

His idea was a simple one, but there was a 90 percent probability that Helen would be separated from him when they put it into practice. And this time there would be no turning back. In the dew-chilled darkness of the crane's engine compartment they faced that probability and accepted it. It was fully understood on both sides that even if he got off the ground—good though his ship would be, even by Earth standards—he might not reach the portal; and if he did reach it, their personal futures would diverge as sharply as those of their native worlds. They had said goodbye.

The plan was for Helen to make her way back to the slideway, unseen from the ship, then approach it in the normal way in full view. Her story was to be that Tallon had forced her to drive him to the city, and that she had been imprisoned after he had contacted the New Wittenburg cell members. Tallon had gone back there when he realized a trap was waiting for him on the *Lyle Star*. She was to give an address in the warehouse belt, and say she had escaped while Tallon and the others were sleeping. Afraid they would be waiting for her near the police stations or out on the streets, she had decided to go to the space terminal, the one place the Earthsiders would avoid. Then she was to tell them about the capsule.

Tallon felt slightly sick when he thought over the flimsy story. He was gambling that Cherkassky would not take time to think, would not even be able to think, when she told him what lay in Tallon's brain. From being a semi-private vendetta on Cherkassky's part, or even a political maneuver by Emm Luther, the incident would explode into the sort of major crisis that topples governments. How things went after that would depend on Cherkassky's reaction. If he high-tailed it into the city, leaving Helen under guard in the ship, Tallon would go aboard and trust to the effectiveness of the vicious little automatic to clear the way for them both to get off the planet. Cherkassky might insist on taking Helen with him as a guide, in which case Tallon would have to try it on his own.

127

Seymour whined and twisted his head away from the ventilation louver, robbing Tallon of his view of the outside. He stroked the wiry head soothingly.

"Take it easy, boy. We'll soon be out of here."

He kept a tight grip on Seymour and held him back up to the narrow slot of light. There was the open ground clearance space at the bottom of the engine housing, and if the dog got out through it he would not want to come back. Tallon did not blame him, but he needed Seymour's eyes more than ever now. It was just about time for Helen to show up among the early morning crews, who were drifting to their jobs. The terminal was coming to life again after the long night, and he got the thought, once more, that somebody might decide to make use of the crane he was in.

Suddenly Seymour's myopic eyes picked up the coppery blur of Helen's hair and a vague green area, which was her uniform.

She went up the ramp and into the *Lyle Star*. Tallon crouched in the darkness, chewing his knuckles, wondering what visible evidence he would get of the success or failure of the gambit. A minute dragged by; then two ... three. ... The time stretched out agonizingly, with no sign of any movement in or around the ship. And then his question was answered!

The sky went dark.

Tallon's heart froze over with dread as he saw what was happening. A formation of six self-propelled guns drifted across the space field less than a hundred feet up, shutting out the light. Dark clouds of earth and stones flapped underneath them, swirling weightlessly in the eddy currents from their negative gravity fields. They fanned out and settled near the northern perimeter of the terminal about half a mile away, and at the same moment sirens screamed their deafening alert. The tiny figures of the technicians who had been moving among the spaceships halted as ululations of the sirens were replaced by a vastly magnified human voice.

This is General Lucas Heller speaking on behalf of the Temporal Moderator. The terminal is now under martial law. All personnel must proceed as quickly as possible to the southern end of the field and muster at the reception area. The entrances have been sealed, and anyone who attempts to leave by any other route will be shot. I repeat: shot. Do not panic, but obey these instructions immediately. This is a planetary emergency.

As the echoes of the voice rolled out across the rows of

ships in flat waves, the sky was darkened again by laser rafts silently taking up positions over the field. Tallon felt his lips drawn out into a quivering, incredulous smile. His gambit had failed—and how it had failed! Cherkassky must have accepted the part of Helen's story about the capsule, and seen through the rest. He must have guessed Tallon was near by and used the ship's radio to proclaim an emergency.

Tallon watched numbly as the space port personnel quit work and took cars or ran to get to the slideway system. Within five minutes the huge field appeared completely lifeless. The only sign of movement was in the swirling dust curtains hanging from the sentient laser rafts.

Nobody had come out of the *Lyle Star* since Helen had gone into it, and he had no way of knowing what had happened to her. Tallon could think of nothing to do except sit quietly in the darkness and wait, although he had nothing to wait for. He pressed his forehead against the cool metal of the engine housing and swore bitterly.

Five more minutes passed; then Tallon heard the sound of feet scraping on concrete. He lifted Seymour up to the louver again, and saw several men in the gray uniforms of the E.L.S.P. coming off the bottom of the ramp. An open military personnel carrier tore along the line of ships and stopped by the group. Most of the men got into it and were driven away toward the city; two others went back up the ramp and disappeared into the ship.

Tallon frowned. It looked as though Cherkassky might be covering Tallon's main bet by checking out the rest of Helen's story, which made Tallon's position doubly hopeless. And when the E.L.S.P. got to the warehouse address and found nothing there, she would be in as deeply as he was. Cherkassky was good, Tallon admitted, fingering the automatic longingly. If only he would come out of the ship, Tallon might be able to get close enough to finish what he had started the night he had shoved Cherkassky out the hotel window. Perhaps that was why he remained in the ship, even though he could no longer expect Tallon to walk into his net.

If he thinks I'm out here ready to risk everything for a last chance to kill him, Tallon thought, what would be his next logical move? Answer: order a thorough search of the area.

As if they had read his mind, the first E.L.S.P. appeared at that moment. They were several hundred yards away as yet, but the fact that he could see several gray uniforms in his limited segment of view meant they must be all over

129

the place. Tallon leaned back against the flanged engine, holding the dog to his chest. There was nothing clever about his hiding place; it would be one of the first places the men would look when they got this far.

Weighing the automatic in his hand, Tallon sat in the darkness, making his decision. He could stay in the compartment until he was cornered, or he could opt to die in the open while making a one-in-a-million bid to get Cherkassky.

"Come on, Seymour," he whispered. "I told you you'd be out of here soon."

He clambered round the engine to reach the inspection hatch, hesitated for a moment, then edged the hatch door open, admitting bright fringes of daylight. He was sliding his foot out through the hatch when he heard the drumming of heavy tires and the whine of an auto engine approaching.

Tallon jerked his foot back and scrambled across the engine compartment again. The sound had come from the personnel carrier. It sped across the open space, braking hard, and slid to a standstill between Tallon and the *Lyle Star*. The same group of E.L.S.P. men leaped out and ran to the ship and up the ramp. In its present position, the vehicle would provide cover for his run to the ship, not that it would do much good, but at least he had no reason to hang back any longer.

"Come on, Seymour. This is it."

Out across the concrete apron a man gave a thin, high-pitched laugh. With a sweet, icy thrill Tallon recognized the voice of Lorin Cherkassky. *Why had he left the ship?* Tallon pressed Seymour's face to the slot, but the dog's eyes kept rolling back and forth, providing only tantalizing flashes of the scene Tallon wanted to see. At last he made out the black-suited, white-collared figure of Cherkassky walking toward the personnel carrier, with Helen and several E.L.S.P. men. Cherkassky seemed to be smiling at her, but Seymour's myopia made it difficult for him to be sure. What in hell, Tallon thought, has *happened?*

Belatedly remembering the eyeset, he flicked the number two stud, which still held Helen's setting, and got behind her eyes, Cherkassky's thin face and incongruously lush wavy hair filled came in view. His eyes were glistening with excitement as he spoke, and Tallon concentrated on his lips, reading the words as they were formed.

". . . appreciate my position, Miss Juste. Your story sounded slightly fantastic under the circumstances; but now that my men have picked up Detainee Tallon at the address you gave us, what can I do but apologize for doubting you? Tallon struggled at first, but when he realized it was no use, he gave up and admitted who he was, so . . ." The view of his face was lost as Helen eyes turned from him to the yellow engine housing where Tallon was hiding.

Tallon wondered if she were as puzzled as he was. The adress Helen had given Cherkassky was one they had picked out of the air, knowing only that it must be somewhere in the warehouse district. But Cherkassky's men had evidently gone to the designated address and found a man they believed to be Sam Tallon. Not only that, but the man actually admitted to being Sam Tallon!

nineteen

Tallon switched back to Seymour's eyes and watched Helen, Cherkassky, and the others approach the personnel carrier. In a few minutes his way to the ship would be clear, thanks to that other Tallon, whose miraculous appearance was utterly mystifying.

However, Cherkassky was going to find out the truth, sooner or later, and when he did nothing would save Helen from his anger. She was walking quietly with the others, apparently unconcerned, but Tallon saw her look toward his hiding place now and then. This was it, he thought—the last time he would ever see her—and all he could do was watch her leave with that monster Cherkassky. In those few seconds Tallon felt himself grow old.

"Helen," he whispered.

At the sound of her name, Seymour twisted violently in Tallon's arms, jumped to the ground, and went scampering across the open space toward the group.

Tallon, still tuned to the dog's eyes, saw the figures expand in his vision. Cherkassky's pinched face turned toward the dog—and Tallon—with a sudden tight look.

As Seymour neared the group he began swerving to get to Helen, and the scene he was transmitting became too unstable to be satisfactory. Tallon reselected Helen's eyes and saw the little dog bounding forward, one of the men waving his arms to shoo Seymour away, and—in the corner of her vision—Cherkassky pointing at the crane and speaking rapidly. Cherkassky's shrill commands filtered into Tallon's hiding place.

Swearing savagely, Tallon lunged across the engine compartment, hampered by not being able to see anything but what Helen was seeing, and burst out through the inspection hatch. He saw his own feet appear under the crane at the far side, as viewed by Helen; then his gray figure appeared, running hard, and heeled sharply as it came round the corner of the base of the bright yellow crane.

Guided by Helen's eyes, Tallon ran desperately toward

132

the ship. His legs were numb from the long wait in the confined space, forcing him to run with a grotesque, stumbling slouch. As he pumped his arms and legs, trying to coax some speed out of them, he saw the men fan out, pulling weapons from their holsters.

He heard the familiar angry whine of hornet guns. The range was a bit too far, and the drug-laden darts clattered about his feet. Then he heard the sound he had been expecting—the flat cracks of pistol fire, followed by distant shouts as the teams of searching troopers heard the commotion. An automatic rifle barked, filling the air with screaming ricochets.

Tallon now saw the small blurred shape of Seymour, frantic with fear, racing toward him. The dog leaped for Tallon's arms, and the impact almost knocked Tallon down. He reeled and kept going, now halfway to the ramp of the *Lyle Star.*

Still through Helen's eyes, he saw Cherkassky run a few steps toward him, then stop and take careful aim with a pistol. On the point of firing, Cherkassky lurched as Helen caught his arm, struggling for the weapon. Cherkassky's face contorted with fury as he shook her off and aimed again. Helen went for him once more, fingers tearing at his face.

Tallon saw white coronas glowing round Cherkassky's eyes as he spun toward her, saw the black round muzzle of the pistol spit flame, saw the darkness flood over Helen's view of his own still-running figure. Then he was blind and snarling with mingled shock and hatred. He reselected Seymour's eyes and saw gray uniforms running toward him—and Cherkassky standing beside Helen's body.

The automatic jarred into Tallon's palm as he turned with it, working the trigger as fast as it would move. Men in gray stumbled and fell under the hail of multiple bullets, but not Cherkassky, who stood there and finally got off a shot at Tallon.

Tallon felt something snatch at his sleeve, heard Seymour give an almost human grunt of pain. Then he was at the foot of the ramp and pounding up the springy slope. The blond sergeant appeared at the top, jaw open with surprise as he fumbled with his holster. Tallon fired instinctively, and the sergeant was lifted right off the ramp as he caught all six bullets.

"Get him, you fools," Cherkassky shouted angrily. "Cut that man down."

Tallon hurtled through the airlock, ducking beneath a

133

hail of lead, and threw over the manual operation lever. As motors whined into life, swinging the heavy outer door into place, Tallon saw men sprinting for the bottom of the ramp. He fired at them, and then the automatic clicked impotently.

Throwing it down, Tallon ran forward and up the short companionway to the control deck, along a corridor, and into the control room. The view screens were blank panels, and the control console was dead. His right hand scuttled down the line of primary switches, bringing life to networks of circuits and systems. There would be a wait of perhaps a minute before the negative gravity units would be ready to drop the ship into the sky. A green light flicked on to indicate that the airlock was closed and the vessel now sealed for flight. Momentarily safe, Tallon slumped into the central seat and activated the view screens, grateful for the Block's meticulous training in the handling of all the basic control configurations.

The screens glowed with color, matching the smaller direct-vision panels, showing him a vista of ships and gantries. He picked out Helen's body near the personnel carrier, lying in the same position, dark green uniform, coppery flash of hair, dark red of spreading blood.

"I'm sorry, Helen," he said aloud. "So very, very sorry."

"Tallon?" A voice crackled from the ceiling near his head. "Is that you, Tallon?"

Tallon could see no grille from which the voice could be coming.

"Yes, this is Sam Tallon," he said warily. "Who are you?"

"This is Fordyce. I wondered if you would get as far as the *Lyle Star.*"

"Fordyce!" Tallon began to understand the enigma of the appearance of the other Tallon. "You've had a bug in here all along!"

"Of course. How else do you think we were able to get a man to that address your girl friend gave Cherkassky? It was a pity you had to tell everybody about the brain capsule, though; it means we can't use that technique any more. The Block would have reprimanded you rather harshly."

"*Would* have?"

"Yes. . . . had you got away. You won't be able to make it, though. There's a squadron of laser rafts right over your head, and Heller has thrown in all the tactical nuclear weapons he had available in the area. You'll never

134

get past that lot; and even if you do, the Grand Fleet will be on your neck before you've cleared the atmosphere."

Tallon was still thinking about Helen Juste. "I guess," he said mechanically, "I've made my share of mistakes this trip."

"I guess." Fordyce's voice was emotionless. "Goodbye, Tallon."

Tallon did not answer. He had just noticed that the E.L.S.P. men outside were running away from the *Lyle Star* as fast as they could. Some of them glanced up at the sky as they ran, which meant the laser rafts were getting ready to use their bright red lances, and that his death was only a matter of seconds now. There would not even be time to get his ship off the ground.

Hopelessly, he reached out with his left hand to initiate the takeoff sequence and noticed that his fingers were streaked with blood, although he had felt no wound. Then he remembered Seymour's cry of pain as they were nearing the ramp. With his other hand he turned the little dog's head to get a close-up of the body. There was a ragged hole in the thorax, just above the rapidly ballooning and contracting belly. The brownish hair was matted with blood.

"You too," Tallon mumbled, feeling Seymour weakly lick his hand.

A blaze of red light flashed on the view screens, and the ship's alarm system shrilled as the laser rafts opened up on the helpless ship. Tallon sat with bowed head for a moment, trying death on for size. Then he did something only a man who was either insane or desperate would do: He reached for the null-space drive panel, knocked off all the safety gates, and punched the jump button.

The leap into another continuum brought instant silence and a searing flash of light from his eyeset. Tallon moaned with agony; then it was all over. The jump was completed.

Outside the ship was the soft, peaceful blackness of a part of the galaxy far beyond mankind's influence. Unfamiliar constellations glowed in the blackness. Tallon did not even try to identify the groupings of brilliant specks; he knew too much about the inimical geometries of null-space.

Because the jump had not been made from one of the established portals, Tallon had hurled himself to a random point in the galactic wheel. He had done it in desperation, but he had done it deliberately, knowing that from those dark immensities there could be no return.

135

twenty

At first there was only a feeling of emptiness, of relief from intolerable pressures and tension. The sensation was similar to the one he'd experienced the night he'd left the Pavilion, but now vastly magnified. He had no identity, and none of the responsibilities of identity. For a time he was nobody, nothing, nowhere—and satisfied with his state of nonexistence. Then part of his mind began to comprehend the horror. Fear slowly permeated his entire being, until Tallon had to clench his teeth to contain it.

There was no way back.

He could make another jump, and another, and another—until his food ran out or he died of old age—the flicker-transits stitching him here and there across the star fields of infinity. But no matter how many random jumps he made, his chances of ever emerging within reach of a habitable planet were still so small as to be virtually nonexistent. As he grew older, sitting in the same chair, he would see almost every manifestation of matter and energy—single stars, binaries, multiples, formless gas clouds, wheels—except that he would, of course, be blind within a few hours.

Tallon snapped out of the descending spiral and turned his attention to Seymour, who was lying in his lap, trembling slightly, curled around the dark wound. The breath-seeking pulsations of his belly were coming more rapidly, but with less vigor. Tallon was pretty sure that Seymour was dying.

He took off his jacket, folded it into a kind of nest on top of the control console for the negative gravity propulsion system, and laid the little dog in it. Seymour was having trouble keeping his eyes open, and Tallon kept getting momentary blackouts. He got up and began to look around for a medical kit, feeling the artificial gravity dragging at his feet. The field was designed to reproduce a man's normal Earth weight, but as it originated right in the floor plates and was subject to the inverse square law, the

136

lower part of the body always felt much heavier than the head and arms.

There were no medical supplies visible anywhere on the control deck within Seymour's restricted view, and to search the other compartments would mean taking Seymour along. Tallon hesitated, undecided. He was going to need food, and it would be better to organize it while he was able to see what he was doing.

"I'm sorry, Seymour," he said. "This'll be your last job."

Tallon gently took the dog up in his arms and moved aft. The *Lyle Star* was basically a conventional freighter, with a half deck in the nose, most of its drive componer' in the tail, and a cylindrical center body for cargo. Its control room, crew quarters, and stores occupied the half deck, and underneath were astrogation equipment, power plants for internal services, and miscellaneous stores. At the rear of the half deck a lateral catwalk looked into the cavernous hold. The rear of the hold was stacked with bales of dried protein plants, but the forward end was clear, the cargo lashing rings neatly tucked into their recesses. Tallon knew the ship was armed, but he could see no evidence of weapon systems and concluded the Block had begun using some very sophisticated stuff since he had last been on one of their ships.

He looked around the little galley, noting that the inventory gauges of the victual supply magazines showed reserves that would last him at least fifteen years. The thought of spending that length of time in darkness and then starving to death was utterly depressing. He hurried out of the galley and began trying other doors, looking briefly into empty rooms.

What an ending, he thought; what a miserable, futile way to finish up. Ever since men had first learned how to boost payloads into space beyond the reach of gravity, they had been littering the cosmos with metal shells containing everything from pans of microbes to nuclear warheads. But an intelligent alien who chanced upon the *Lyle Star* would find the most baffling piece of cosmic garbage yet—a man with brown plastic buttons for eyes and a dying dog in his arms, wandering around an empty ship. No alien was going to come aboard, however, because none of the millions of stellar probes had ever found evidence of intelligent . . .

Clang-ang-ang-ng-ng! Metal collided with metal somewhere near the airlock. The echoes faded away in the vast spaces of the hold.

Tallon's knees almost buckled as the shock wave surged along his nerves. He was in a narrow corridor whose aft end opened on the catwalk skirting the hold, and he would be able to see what had caused the sound by going to the end and looking over the handrail. Tallon walked toward the dark rectangle, then stepped out onto the catwalk. A black shape was moving on the lower deck, close to the inner door of the lock.

It was Lorin Cherkassky.

He looked up, and Tallon saw that he had a bloody gash on his forehead and that he was still holding a pistol. They faced each other in silence for several throbbing seconds. Cherkassky gave a prim, icy smile, his head making slight rocking movements on the long turkey neck. Tallon involuntarily took a step back.

"*There* you are, Tallon," Cherkassky said amiably. "And with your little friend, too."

"Don't try to come up here." Tallon said it for lack of anything else to say.

Cherkassky shrank back against the metal wall, still smiling. "Tallon, you and I have met only twice before—and each time you have attempted to kill me. If your final shot had been an inch lower, I would be dead right now."

"It wasn't my final shot," Tallon lied.

"In that case you were very foolish to lose your gaudy little pistol. I suppose you heard me kick it down into the hold? If I had realized it was loaded I'd have been more careful in case it——"

"All right, Cherkassky. You're laying it on too thick. It shows lack of taste."

He stepped quickly back into the corridor, wondering what he could use to defend himself. The only possibility was to find something to throw. He ran to the galley and feverishly opened cupboards and drawers with his free hand. There were no carving knives, and the table knives were of lightweight plastic. Seconds were racing by, and to make matters even worse, Seymour's eyes were almost closed, reducing Tallon's vision to a hazy grayness.

The only objects that looked promising were several large cans of fruit next to one of the supply magazines. He tried to lift them in one arm, but they rolled away, clattering on the floor. Tallon set Seymour on the floor, gathered up the cans, and ran blindly down the corridor toward the control room, expecting at any instant to feel a lead slug smash into his spine. He got into the control

138

room, jumped to one side, and fumbled with the eyeset's controls until he picked up Cherkassky's eyes.

He got a sharp, steady view of the corridor, as seen from the other end, and he realized Cherkassky had stood on the catwalk and watched him run, without shooting. That meant the little man was determined to make a marathon out of it. Tallon hefted one of the heavy cans, edged across to the doorway, and hurled the can down the corridor with all his strength. Through Cherkassky's eyes he saw his hand appear and the can come barreling through the air. Cherkassky avoided it with ease and it bounced noisily into the hold, filling the ship with echoes.

Tallon groped on the floor and got another can. He decided to wait till Cherkassky was farther along the corridor, giving him less time to see—and avoid—the improvised missile thrown at him. With his back pressed against the wall, Tallon watched the slowly zooming view of the corridor and the expanding rectangle of the control-room door. At the entrance to the galley, the view rotated to take in the disordered cupboards and drawers; and there was Seymour inching across the floor, his pointed teeth bared in a ridiculous attempt at a snarl. Tallon guessed what was coming next.

"Go back, Seymour!" he shouted. "Lie down, boy."

Apart from shouting, there was nothing he could do. Closing his eyelids did nothing to blot out the pictures he was receiving. He had to stand and look along the pistol sights with Cherkassky's eyes. The pistol roared, and Seymour's body smashed against the far wall of the galley.

Tallon stepped out and threw the can, every muscle in his body snapping taut behind it. He heard a thud as it connected with something soft, and then he was winging down the corridor, propelled by a white-hot thrust of hatred. The metal walls spun violently as he slammed into Cherkassky. They half-skidded, half-rolled, right to the dark edge of the catwalk, then rebounded from the handrail and back down the full length of the corridor. Somewhere along the way the eyeset was pushed up on to his forehead, and Tallon was unable to see, but it made no difference to him. He was at grips with Cherkassky, and a loudly chanting voice in his head was telling him that nothing in the whole universe could stop his hands from doing their appointed work.

He was wrong.

Using the Block-developed combat rhythms, he might have extinguished Cherkassky in a few seconds; but his fingers, obeying a more ancient discipline, crooked into the other man's throat. He felt Cherkassky's body transformed by the same steely strength it had displayed when they were falling from the hotel window long ago. Cherkassky's locked forearms triangled upward in the oldest counter in the book, splitting Tallon's hold, and Cherkassky twisted free. Tallon tried to prevent the separation, which would give Cherkassky the advantage, but blows from the heavy pistol numbed Tallon's arms. He was forced to take a valuable second to pull the eyeset down onto his nose, knowing as he did so that the fight was lost.

Cherkassky made use of this opportunity, and Tallon recovered vision just in time to see the gun barrel being jammed into his solar plexus. He fell backward into the control room, the wind knocked out of him. Once again he looked along the sights of Cherkassky's pistol, this time at himself. The point of aim wandered from his belly to his head and back down again.

"You've had a long run, Tallon," Cherkassky said quietly, "but in a way I'm glad. Shooting any other prisoner would ruin my reputation with our revered Moderator, but you've caused so much trouble that nobody is going to complain."

Tallon, gasping for breath, made a weak attempt to roll sideways as he saw Cherkassky's finger tighten on the trigger; then the underlying assumption behind the words reached his brain, a final message of unexpected hope.

"Wait ... wait ..." His lungs fought to supply the air necessary for speech.

"Goodbye, Tallon."

"Wait, Cherkassky ... there's something you don't— look at the screens!"

Cherkassky's eyes flicked momentarily to the unfamiliar star patterns on the black panels, back down to Tallon, then focused on the screens again.

"This is a trick," Cherkassky said in a voice that was not quite normal. "You didn't ..."

"I did. We made an open-ended jump." Tallon struggled for breath. "So you were right when you said shooting me won't ruin your reputation. Nobody will ever know, Cherkassky."

"You're lying. The screens could be showing a recorded view."

"Look at the direct-vision panels then. How do you think we got into space through all that heavy stuff you called in?"

140

"They knew I was in the ship. They wouldn't fire with me in the ship."

"They fired," Tallon said flatly, "and we jumped."

"But they *wouldn't*," Cherkassky whispered. "*Not at me.*"

Tallon kicked his feet upward, doubling Cherkassky forward on top of him. This time he fought coldly and efficiently, impervious to fear or hatred, to the thunderous sound of the pistol, to the knowledge that his enemy's living eyes were his sole remaining gateway to light and beauty and stars.

Tallon closed that gateway forever.

twenty-one

You can feel like dying. You can even lie down on the floor and will yourself to die. But all that happens is you go right on living.

Tallon made the discovery slowly, over a period of hours, as he walked the silent ship. He visualized the *Lyle Star* as a bubble of brilliance suspended in an infinity of darkness, and himself as a fleck of darkness drifting in a sharply confined universe of light. Nothing could be more pointless than prolonging that arrangement for fifteen years; yet he was hungry, and there was food, so why not eat?

Tallon thought it over. A short-term goal. Once it was achieved, what then? Wrong type of thinking, he decided. If you are going to exist on short-term goals, you discard the logical processes associated with long-term goals. When you are hungry you cook something and you eat it. Then maybe you get tired, so you sleep; and when you wake up you are hungry again. . . .

He took off the eyeset, but found his plastic eyes felt uncomfortably naked without their protective covering, and put it back on. The first short-term goal of his new existence would be to set up a tidy house. He found Cherkassky's limp body, dragged it to the airlock, and propped it against the outer door. It took him several minutes to position the body in such a way that it would be sure to be carried clear of the lock when the residual air exhausted. A dead body made a poor traveling companion under normal circumstances, but an exposure to zero pressure would make it even less attractive.

When he was satisfied with the arrangement of the body he went to fetch Seymour, and laid the pathetic little husk in Cherkassky's lap.

Back in the control room he identified the relevant controls by touch, then blew the lock. Exit two more characters, he thought, leaving Sam Tallon alone on the stage. Doc Winfield had been the first; then Helen, with the red hair and whiskey-colored eyes. It occurred to him

142

that she might not be dead, but there was no way he could find out, and he was straying into the wrong type of thinking again.

Tallon went to the galley, lifted one can from each supply magazine, and opened them. He identified their contents and memorized where each had come from in the row of dispensers. As a welcome change from fish, he decided on steak, and while it was cooking he found a refrigerated compartment with stacks of plastic tubular containers of beer. Thankful that Parane, where the *Lyle Star* had originated, had both adequate protein supplies and a sensible outlook on the use of alcohol, he settled down to his first meal in alien space. When he was finished he disposed of the plastic plates and utensils, then sat down and waited for nothing to happen.

Some time later he grew tired and went to find a bed. Sleep was a long time in coming because he was many thousands of light-years from the rest of his kind.

Tallon kept it up for four cycles of activity and sleep before concluding he was bound to go mad if he continued this way. He decided he had to have a long-term goal to give his life direction, even if the term were longer than his life span and the goal unattainable.

He went into the control room and explored the central computing bank with his fingertips, wishing he had paid more attention to it while eyes were still available to him. It took him some time to satisfy himself that it was a standard type, based on the cybernetic intelligence amplifier. Null-space travel demanded that a ship position itself within portals measuring no more than two light-seconds across. The standards of precision involved required that the computing facility and the astrogation complex be unified into a single automatic control system.

The control complex was fully programed to account for variants, such as variable magnitude stars, in the perceived celestial sphere; but provision was also made to prevent positional fixes from being affected by rare and unpredictable phenomena like novas and supernovas. This took the form of data injection panels that provided pathways right into, among other things, the instruction store. The data injector had not changed since the first days of null-space travel. Tallon had heard that the relatively primitive system was retained solely because it enabled a reasonably competent engineer to convert a spaceship into an interstellar probe.

In other words, the design philosophy of the constructors was: This vessel is fully guaranteed and will always get you to your destination; but if it doesn't, you might as well try finding another world while you are out there.

Tallon had never investigated the matter personally, but he was banking on the stories being true, for there was no point in his making any further jumps without some means of checking on his position. The possibilities of his getting within reach of a habitable world in fifteen years of continuous null-space leaps were perhaps one in a billion. He was not deceiving himself about the chances of success, but there was nothing else open to him; and vegetating, which he had tried for four days, was unacceptable. Besides, in a truly random universe, he might make only one jump and find himself hanging above Earth itself, almost able to breathe its atmosphere, to smell the smoke of leaf fires drifting in the soft thick air of October evenings. . . .

He went to work on the central control complex. Two more days of rest and activity went by before he was satisfied that he had successfully reprogramed the system to meet his new requirements. Working blind, he taxed his brain to its full extent, reaching the same degree of involvement that had enabled him to produce the eye-sets.

Several times he found himself filled with a powerful sense of satisfaction. This, he thought, is what I'm good at. Why did I give up everything after college and take to star-jumping? Each time, unaccountably, he saw Helen's red hair and unusual eyes superimposed on his mental picture of the control complex. And finally he had altered the astrogation network from a beast that would jump only when it knew where it was, to one that would refuse to move if its multiple senses detected a planetary system within reach.

When Tallon had finished he felt sane. His mind felt sharp and clear. He went to bed and slept soundly.

After breakfast, which was what he called the first meal after a period of sleep, Tallon made his way into the control room and sat down in the center seat. He hesitated, preparing himself for the psychic wrench, and hit the button that projected the ship into that other incomprehensible universe. *Click!* A flash of unbearable brilliance seared into his eyes; then the jump was over.

Tallon ripped off the eyeset and lay back in the big chair with his hands pressed over his eyes, his mind racing. He had forgotten the flash that had burned into his optic nerves when he'd jumped the *Lyle Star* out of New

Wittenburg. There was nothing in any book that dealt with light flashes occurring in null-space; in fact most people experienced a momentary blindness during the transition. He listened to the computer and it was quiet, which meant he had not materialized within range of any planet in any part of the big, cold galaxy.

Mentally shrugging, he prepared to make another jump. This time he lowered the eyeset's sensitivity to almost zero, and when the flash came it was greatly reduced in intensity. He took the eyeset off and made another jump that produced no light at all. With the eyeset back on, he made a fourth jump, and the flash was there again.

Tallon began to get excited, without knowing why. The flash was associated with the eyeset—that much seemed certain. But what was causing it? Was there some form of radiation in null-space that the eyeset was picking up? Hardly, because the circuits were designed to screen out anything except the incredibly subtle "phasing-of-phases" emanations from glial cells. What else then? There were no people in the null-space continuum.

Tallon got up from the seat and began to pace the control room—eight steps to the wall, turn, eight steps back.

He remembered the conversation with Helen Juste about her brother's work for the Emm Luther probe-design center. Carl Juste had been working on an idea that the null-space universe might be extremely small, perhaps only a matter of yards in diameter. Could the reason no normal radio equipment ever worked in null-space (thus preventing humans from mapping its topography) be that they swamped themselves in their own signals, the troughs in the wave profiles filling up as they traveled endlessly around the tiny universe? If that were so, then the human eye—which transmitted its information not by amplitude, frequency, or even phase modulation, but by phasing of phases—could very well be the only piece of "electronic" equipment capable of operating in null-space without completely obliterating its own signal characteristics. And the eyeset could be the first receiver to work in null-space. But the question remained: What was causing the flash?

Tallon stopped short as the answer hit him: There *were* people in the null-space universe! The time taken for the warp generators to set up their field and collapse it again was less than two seconds on a minimum increment jump, but the trade lanes of the empire were busy. Millions of tons of freight and passengers passed through the zigzag

145

routes of galactic commerce every hour, so at any given instant there were thousands of human beings in the null-space continuum. The blurring effect, caused by the signal repetition in the claustrophobic universe, could be enough to unite all their optic-nerve emanations into one vast, unorchestrated output.

He felt his heart pound with excitement. The glial-cell emanations were so weak as to be practically nonexistent. It was just possible they could cross the null-space universe only a few times before dying out, which meant there might well be directional information in the flash they produced in the eyeset—to say nothing of the possibility of a form of null-space travel controlled by human will instead of by the dictates of an alien geometry.

Tallon stood still for a moment. Then he started down the corridor heading for the *Lyle Star's* maintenance workshop.

After a few minutes of fumbling among the tool racks, Tallon managed to identify a heavy power saw with a conventional reciprocating blade. He chose it in preference to a laser saw, on which it would be too easy for a blind man to lose his fingers.

Carrying the saw on his shoulder, he went to the stern of the ship, skirting the bales of compressed protein plant, and went to work on the first layer of radiation screening. He cut three panels, each measuring five feet by two feet, from the inch-thick material; then cut a smaller one, two-feet square. The metal-seeded plastic was cumbersome, and he fell several times while getting it up to the control deck.

With the screens in position, he made several attempts to use a multiwelder on them, but his blindness was too much of a handicap. Putting the welder aside, he made crude angle brackets by flattening and bending empty food cans, and bolted them to the plastic panels. The work took a long time—even a familiar hand drill became a tricky thing to use without sight—but in the end he had constructed something like a sentry box. He changed the bit in the drill and bored a single pinhole in the central wall of the box.

Tallon's heart sank when he tried to move the box to where he wanted it and felt its uncompromising weight. He levered it unsuccessfully for a few minutes before remembering he was in a spaceship, an environment in which weight was a contrived luxury. He found the master switch for the artificial gravity system and turned it off, and the box was a lot easier to handle. He positioned it in front of the captain's chair, with the hollow side facing aft, and turned the gravity on again.

Hoping for success and fearing disappointment, Tallon clambered over the central chair and worked himself forward into the box. The open side was almost in contact with the footrest of the chair, and when he knelt on the square of deck enclosed by the box's three walls he was effectively screened from the direct-vision panels. He put his right hand around the side of the box, drew the null-space drive console close to him, and found the jump button. With his left hand he located the pinhole—now the only channel by which optic-nerve signals could reach him—and positioned his eyes directly behind it.

This time when he hit the jump button the flash was— as he had hoped—no more than a sudden brief glow of bearable intensity. Now it was time for the crucial test. He made a series of jumps, being careful to keep his head in the same relationship to the pinhole; then he got out of the box, grinning with satisfaction. The flashes had varied in intensity.

Ignoring his insistent hunger pangs, Tallon de-activated the null-space drive unit, and threw the warp generators over to manual control. The *Lyle Star* was now set up to make extended visits to the null-space universe without altering its position in either plane of existence.

Tallon detached a simple numerical computing module from the main installation and spent some time familiarizing himself with its keyboard, working to recover the old and almost forgotten skill by which his fingers made the instrument an extension of his brain. When he was ready he visualized himself as being at the center of a hollow sphere, and he assigned basic coordinates to two thousand regularly spaced points on the sphere's inner surface.

The next step of the project was to rotate the *Lyle Star* about its three major axes, lining up the prow with every point in turn. At each position he made the transit into null-space, estimated on a simple arbitrary scale the brightness of the signal he was receiving, then came back and fed the information into the computer.

He had to stop for sleep three times before it was finished, but in the end he had in his hands—pitifully incomplete though it was—man's first map of the null-space universe.

Precisely, it was a low-definition computer model of the disposition of the galactic trade lanes, as seen from one point in null-space. What he needed now was a similar model of the normal-space universe as seen from the same point. With that, he could turn both over to the big computer and let it draw a comparison. There were nineteen worlds in the empire, and as the initial and terminal portals for all but two of them were close to Earth, the normal-space model would show a marked concentration in that region. The null-space map would not show an identical concentration, as there was not a one-to-one correspondence between the two continuums, but Tallon hoped a computer would find *some* correlation between the two. And if it did—he was home, in more than one sense.

As a kind of hubristic celebration, he decided to treat himself to a fine meal while thinking over the next step. He cooked an extra large steak and began methodically reducing his stock of beer. When he had eaten he sat quietly on a stool in the galley and assessed the situation. He had done pretty well without eyes so far, but that was because he was tackling familiar problems with instruments he could handle almost by instinct. Building up a computer model of his own normal-space universe would, paradoxically, be more difficult. He would not be able to "see" the density of the interwoven space routes, and the alternative was to feed in the galactic coordinates of every portal. This would be a big job—the journey from Emm Luther to Earth, for example, would involve feeding in three coordinates for every one of the eighty thousand portals. It could be done, of course—the data would be in storage somewhere—but without eyes, the going would be . . . rough. The word "impossible" had sprung into his mind and been thrust aside.

Tallon drank steadily, feeling his earlier elation subside. Because of his blindness it looked as though he would have to explore the main computing facility, taking it apart and assembling it again in the dark, merely to get to know it. Then he would have to listen to everything in its random access memory, until he obtained the data he needed. That could take five or ten years. He could starve to death before he accomplished what a sighted man, able to read the computer's language, could do in hours.

Tallon began to doze, but was awakened by a furtive, squeaking noise he had not heard for many years. He froze for a moment before identifying the sound. He was listening to a descendant of the first stowaway that had

148

ever slipped on board a ship back in the dawn ages when man was pitting his first flimsy ships against the seas of Earth.

It was a rat.

twenty-two

Tallon had forgotten there were no lights shining in the cargo hold. He found the lighting panel on the control deck and clicked on every tube in the ship, but even with the eyeset at full gain he picked up nothing. This, he concluded, was because there was too much screening between him and the rat, or because the rat was hiding beyond the reach of light. Either or both of these factors had prevented him from discovering the animal before it came forward in search of food.

He went out of the control room and along the central corridor. Standing at the handrail of the transverse catwalk he detected something, not so much a glimmer of light as a slight lessening of darkness. It was a new type of problem. He had not only to adjust to having his eyes separated from his body, but also to deduce exactly where his eyes were, from very slender clues.

The rat was probably somewhere in the bales of protein plant, but remembering how quickly it had vanished when he'd grabbed for it in the galley, Tallon felt there was no point in shifting the cargo. He decided to set a nonlethal trap.

There was the old trick of upending a box, tilting it with a short stick propped under one side, and jerking the support away when the quarry was underneath. He changed his mind about it when he recalled a boyhood experiment that had resulted in an unexpectedly speedy mouse being flattened by an edge of the box. In the present circumstances, the rat, which had probably crept aboard at Parane, was more valuable than a champion racehorse.

Tallon took some bread from the galley, put it down near the bales of cargo, and lay down close by. He closed his eyes and pretended to sleep. As the minutes dragged by he found himself dozing off. He fought it determinedly for a while; then he began to notice a gradual increase in brightness. There was a shifting of dim planes, areas of patchy grayness emerged from the darkness, followed by an irregular area of brightness like the mouth of a cave. A huge shape stirred near by, frighteningly; red eyes gleamed, speculatively and coldly. Tallon kept his breathing steady. He knew that his rat had merely passed close to another rat on its way out of their lair.

Quite suddenly he could see bright metal floor plates from close up, stretching away toward dark horizons like a lifeless desert. There was an alien sky above, a suggestion of cavernous vastness. The interior of the hold, as viewed by a rat, was an alien and unfriendly universe in which the natural instinct was to run for the safety of dark corners, for the solace of red-eyed mates in the black caves.

Tallon wondered, uneasily, if the eyeset might be a more effective receiver than he had imagined. What if there were a link-up between the signals fed to the visual cortex and the other mental processes of the animal or person concerned, a kind of emotional overlap? Perhaps if he tuned in on a bull that was looking at a waving cloth he would pick up undertones of anger. Perhaps using Cherkassky's eyes had made him a ruthless killer, an instrument that turned the little man's own feral instincts back on himself in a new manifestation of poetic justice. In that case, had Helen's eyes brought him love?

Absorbed with this idea, Tallon barely noticed the little mound of bread come into view as the rat neared it. The mound got nearer, became a tumbled mountainside of food; then his own gigantic, bearded, dreaming face loomed on the threatening horizon. The scene froze for a long time, and Tallon forced himself to remain motionless. Finally the rat began to advance again. Tallon waited until the glistening cellular structure of the bread was very close before springing forward. Seen through the rat's eyes, his attempt to snatch it was almost laughable.

At the first movement of the slumbering giant's tree-trunk fingers everything blurred, and he was back in the half-world of dimly seen shapes. He tried three more times, with the same result, before admitting to himself that he would have to find a better way. What happens, he thought, if I can't catch it? The tableau becomes even more ridiculous. In the metal bubble of light and air a man with plastic eyes crawls in endless pursuit of a rodent, never catching it because the only time he can see it is when it sees him. . . .

"If a good swordsman challenges you to a duel," Tallon said aloud, "you insist on fighting with pistols."

The sound of his voice in the lonely stillness of the ship

reminded him that he was, after all, a human being, a member of the species whose special weapon was thought, something it was disturbingly easy to forget while his eyes crept in darkness under the cargo.

He picked up the bread and carried it forward, setting it on the plates at the end of the control-deck corridor. He stopped for a moment in the galley, then went on into the control room and sat down. This time Tallon waited until the rat was nose-deep in the mountain of food before he made his move.

He switched off the artificial gravity.

As the struggling, shrilling rat floated into the air Tallon swam toward it, ready with a transparent plastic jar taken from the galley. At the sight of him the rat became frantic, whipping its body about in the air like a landed fish, presenting Tallon—who got only fragmentary, whirling glimpses of himself—with a delicate problem in ballistics. On the second attempt he scooped up the writhing animal, put the lid loosely back on the jar, and moved forward again, smiling slightly as the plastic container vibrated in his hand.

The first thing Tallon did with his new eyes was to instruct the *Lyle Star* to find out where it was.

It took the astrogation complex only a few seconds to take crude bearings from the other seventeen galaxies of the home cluster, then refine and confirm its findings with quasar readings. The ship was about 10,000 light-years from the galactic center, and about 35,000 light-years from Earth. Tallon was a hardened star tramp, but it was difficult to look at the glowing figures hanging in the air above the computer without an icy sense of dismay. The distance across which he hoped to pick his way was so great that the light from Sol could not reach him; it would have been absorbed by interstellar dust on the way. But if there were no dust, and if he had a telescope of unlimited power and resolution, he could have looked at Earth and seen Upper Paleolithic men beginning to assert supremacy over the forests of Earth, proudly carrying their newly perfected weapons of flint.

Tallon tried to visualize himself successfully crossing that unimaginable void—seated in the big chair, plastic button eyes blind to the flowing starscapes, a captive rat blinking malevolently in a plastic jar on Tallon's knees— guided only by an idea born in blindness in his own mind and now spinning endlessly in the brain cells of a computer.

Fantastic as the vision was, he had to go ahead and try.

To build his model of the space routes, Tallon transferred the position of every portal, expressed as absolute coordinates, into the computer's working volume and converted them to coordinates based on the *Lyle Star's* present position. This took some time, but it gave him a map that was the normal-space equivalent of the one he already had of null-space. He then plugged the module containing the latter back into the main facility and programed it to find the correspondence, if any existed. There was also the possibility that there was a genuine correspondence so attenuated that it would be found only by one of the planet-wide computer networks such as existed on Earth, but he refused to dwell on that.

An hour later the computer chimed softly and a set of equations was born in the air above it, the glowing symbols hanging silently over its solution projector. There was no necessity for Tallon to understand it—the astrogation complex was capable of absorbing and acting on the information by itself—but he had a natural interest in seeing for himself what could very well be the mathematical touchstone that would convert null-space lead to normal-space gold.

For a moment the equations looked completely incomprehensible, as though he were taking them in with not only a rat's eyes but a rat's brain as well. He stared at the figures, holding the plastic jar up in front of them, then they seemed to shift into focus as his dormant mathematical facilities were stirred into activity. Tallon recognized the elements of a four-dimensional wave surface, the quartic, and suddenly realized he was looking at an incomplete and camouflaged definition of a Kummer surface. That meant null-space was analogous to a second-degree singularity surface—a knobbly interconnected entity, with sixteen real nodes and as many double tangent planes. No wonder then that, with a negligible sample of referent points, the years of research into null-space astrogation had got precisely nowhere.

Tallon smiled. If he got out of his present situation, and it turned out that the nineteenth-century German mathematician Ernst Kummer had been a Lutheran, there would be a beautiful piece of irony involved.

Tallon reconnected the astrogation complex and the null-space drive unit, and punched in the coordinates and jump increment for what he hoped would be the first controlled flight in the history of interstellar travel. He took off the eyeset, to avoid a prolonged blast of light, and hurled the ship into the null-space continuum for the eight seconds demanded by the new equations.

When he put the eyeset on again he sat and sweated for a moment before lifting the rat up to where it could see the position report of the astrogation complex. It presented a long string of absolute coordinates that Tallon was too agitated to comprehend. He instructed the computer to reduce the information to give a single, simple figure: the geodesic distance between the *Lyle Star* and Earth.

The new answer was just short of a hundred light-years.

Assuming he had not made a lucky random jump, that would mean an error of only one third of a percent of the total distance.

Trembling slightly, in a manner unbecoming to the conqueror of null-space, Tallon programed the next jump and carried it out. This time when he put on the eyeset there was a sharp bright star glowing ahead. The computer said less than half a light-year.

Tallon cheered unashamedly and squeezed the plastic jar, wishing he could convey to its uncomprehending inmate that the shining jewel in front of them was the sun that had lighted the way for both their ancestors to crawl out of the sea, and that their breathing bodies had been created from its abundant energy, that it represented everything summed up in the word "home." Never mind, he thought, no doubt you and that other rat back there are thinking things I'll never be able to understand either.

He made another jump, aware that this could be the last before going over to ion drive. When it was completed, Tallon raised the eyeset, knowing that he must be well into the solar system, possibly within sight of Earth itself.

Before he could settle the eyeset on the bridge of his nose, the raucous note of an alarm hooter blasted through the control room.

"Identify yourself immediately," a harsh voice crackled from the external communications system. "Reply at once, or you will be destroyed by missiles that have already been launched toward your position." The voice went on, repeating the message in the other major languages of the empire.

Tallon sighed wearily. He had crossed half the galaxy; and now he knew, beyond all doubt, that he had reached home.

twenty-three

"This is your last warning. Identify yourself immediately."

Tallon activated the communications system. "Let's do things a little differently for once," he said. "Why don't *you* identify yourself?"

There was a silence, and when the voice spoke again it contained a faintly noticeable edge of indignation. "I will repeat this warning only once: Missiles have already been dispatched toward your position."

"Save them," Tallon said casually, resting his fingers on the null-space jump button. "They can't touch me. And *I* repeat: I want to know your name and rank."

Another silence. Tallon leaned back in the big chair. He knew he was being unnecessarily awkward, but those 35,000 light-years had drained him of the last vestiges of tolerance for the politico-military system in which he had spent most of his life. While waiting for a reply he programed the *Lyle Star* to make a jump through null-space of only half a million miles, and held it in reserve. He had just finished when preliminary flickers of color wavered in the air in front of him, showing that communications techs somewhere were laboring to establish visual contact with his ship.

The colors brightened abruptly and flowed together to form a three-dimensional image of a hard-faced, gray-haired man in the charcoal uniform of a marshal. He was seated, and the image was so good that Tallon could see the network of tiny red veins over his cheekbones. The marshal leaned forward, with disbelief in his eyes.

"Name, please," Tallon said determinedly, making no concessions for the effect his appearance was bound to have on the marshal.

"I don't know who you are," the marshal said slowly, "but you have just committed suicide. Our missiles have almost reached range coincidence. It's too late to stop them now."

Tallon smiled easily, enjoying a moment of megalomania; and as the proximity indicators screamed he hit the jump button. A flood of brilliance poured into his eyes, but it was only the now-familiar null-space flash. When the *Lyle Star* emerged in normal space again one of the vision panels was glowing fiercely with the missile bursts half a million miles away. The image of the marshal had vanished, but it wavered into apparent solidity a few seconds later. He looked amazed.

"How did you do that?"

"Name, please."

"I am Marshal James J. Jennings, commanding the Third Echelon of the Grand Fleet of Imperial Earth." The marshal shifted uneasily in his seat; he had the look of a man swallowing a bitter pill.

"Please listen to this carefully, Marshal; here's what I want you to do."

"What makes you——"

"Please keep quiet and listen," Tallon interrupted coldly. "I'm Sam Tallon, formerly of the Amalgamated Intelligence Agencies, and I'm piloting the *Lyle Star,* which was sent to Emm Luther to pick me up. You can confirm this easily enough."

The marshal leaned to one side, listening to something that was not being transmitted through the intership hookup. He nodded several times and turned to face Tallon.

"I have just checked on it. The *Lyle Star* was directed to Emm Luther, but it ran into difficulties. Someone on the ship made an open-ended jump, with Tallon aboard—which means you are lying."

Tallon spoke angrily. "I've come a long way, Marshal, and I'm——" He stopped as Jennings suddenly left his chair, disappearing from view for a few seconds, then came back.

"It's all right, Tallon," the marshal said with a new note of respect in his voice. "We have just managed to get a visual check on your ship. It is the *Lyle Star.*"

"Are you certain? I could have painted the name on it myself."

Jennings nodded. "That's true, but we weren't going by the name. Don't you know you have a complete berthing cradle and a few thousand yards of spaceport concrete with you? There are a couple of dead men in Lutheran uniforms drifting around you, too."

Tallon had forgotten that the *Lyle Star* would have snatched a sizable chunk of Emm Luther into null-space inside its warp field. The instantaneous vacuum created by the ship's departure must have caused havoc in that region of the terminal. And Helen's body had been right on the edge of it. His need for her, which had been blurred by danger and despair, was suddenly sharp, obliterating everything else in his mind. *Oh, that I were where Helen lies. . . .*

"I must apologize to you, Tallon," Jennings said. "A state of war has existed between Earth and Emm Luther for three days. That's why we were so jumpy when your ship was detected so close to Earth and so far from a portal. It looked like some kind of sneak attack."

"Don't apologize, Marshal. Can you arrange a direct communications link with the Block? Right now?"

"I could, but it wouldn't be secure."

"That doesn't matter. I have nothing private to say at the moment."

"We are delighted that you got back, Tallon, but this is highly irregular." The representative of the Block was a man Tallon had never seen before. His fresh skin, stubby brown hands, and casual clothes made him look like a successful small-time farmer. The background to his image was a deliberately anonymous pastel green blur.

"Irregular, but also important," Tallon said. "Are you near the top?"

The man raised his bleak eyes for a second, and Tallon knew he was near the top. "My name is Seely. Before you say anything, Tallon, I want to remind you we are on an open circuit. I also want——"

"Let's stop talking about irrelevancies," Tallon said impatiently, "and concentrate on my requirements."

"Tallon!" Seely half-rose from his seat, then relaxed into it again. He smiled. "We will terminate this conversation right now. Obviously, you have been under a great strain, and there is a possibility you might stray on to classified subjects. I'm sure you know what I mean."

"You mean I might make some accidental reference to the capsule in my brain? The one that still holds all the route information for getting to the new Lutheran planet?"

The ruddy brown of Seely's cheeks changed to the color of clay. "I'm sorry you did that, Tallon. I'll talk to you here in the Block. Marshal Jennings has been instructed to bring you in without any further delay. That's all."

"Marshal Jennings can't do that," Tallon said quickly and confidently. "Ask him what happened when he fired some of his missiles at me half an hour ago."

Seely moved a key on his desk, cutting off the sound,

and spoke silently to someone out of camera range. He switched on the sound again and turned to Tallon, his eyes wary. "I've been hearing some unusual reports about you, Tallon. The first indications are that your ship emerged in normal space right inside the solar system. Have you established a new portal?"

"Portals are a thing of the past, Seely. I've cracked the null-space astrogation problem. I can go anywhere I want without portals."

Seely interlaced his stubby fingers and stared at Tallon over the steeple they formed. "In that case, I have no alternative but to order a complete interference blanket over all communications in the solar system until we bring you in to make your report."

"You do that," Tallon said pleasantly, "and you'll never see me again. I will visit every world in the empire, starting with Emm Luther, and broadcast the method on every waveband there is."

"How do you expect to get out? I can englobe every . . ." Seely hesitated.

"Every portal, I believe you were going to say," Tallon put in, feeling a cold anger flooding through him. "You are out of date, Seely; you and the portals and the Block are all part of ancient history. From now on we are through squabbling over a handful of worlds found by pure chance. Every planet in the galaxy is open to us, and there is going to be room for everybody. Even for you and your kind, Seely—although you'll have to change. Nobody is going to stay and play soldiers in your backyard when a hundred thousand new planets are available out there for *living* on.

"Now—are you going to listen to me, or do I say goodbye? I've wasted too much time here already." Tallon poised his hand over the red null-space jump button. The ship had not been programed for a controlled jump from its present position, so hitting the button could flick the *Lyle Star* right across the Rim; but—he felt a surge of savage pleasure—that no longer mattered.

Seely looked hunted. "All right, Tallon. What do you want?"

"Three things: An immediate cancellation of all preparations for hostilities against Emm Luther; clearance for me to broadcast details of the null-space astrogation technique to anybody who wants to use it; and I want to commandeer Marshal Jennings' flagship for an immediate flight to Emm Luther."

Seely opened his mouth to reply, but a new voice cut into the circuit: "Requests granted."

158

Tallon recognized the voice of Caldwell Dubois, statutory representative of Earth and the four other human settlements of the solar system.

The mirrored, thousand-yard keel of the *Wellington*, flagship of Space Marshal Jennings, glinted frostily in the thin air high above New Wittenburg. It had become the second ship to make a controlled null-space flight and the first to do so from Earth to Emm Luther. An hour had elapsed since its powerful transmitters had sphered their message downward across the broad face of the planet.

The *Wellington* was too huge for even the largest berthing cradles in the New Wittenburg terminal, and so had chosen to remain aloft—though not in orbit—in a prodigious but peaceful display of sheer power. An elliptical section of its hull detached itself from the rest of the ship and drifted downward, revealing itself to be a flat-bottomed lifeboat.

Tallon stood at the lifeboat's main view screen, watching the long single continent expand beneath him. He was still wearing the eyeset, but during the approach to Emm Luther and the subsequent broadcast, the unlimited technical resources of the *Wellington's* electronics shops had fitted it with a pea-sized television camera and coded its output in accordance with Tallon's original plan. He had his own eyes again, providing him with good, though monocular, vision. Later, he had been assured, they would be able to give him a camera built right into each eye.

The twilit continent curved away below, dull greens and ochres sifted through each other, edged with lacy white where they met the tideless ocean. Tallon could take in almost the whole of his night walk in one glance—that long straggling line leading north through invisibly fine details such as the mist-hidden Pavilion and the swamp; the city of Sweetwell and The Persian Cat; the probe factory, where he had been wounded; Carl Juste's estate; and the mountain motel where he had spent five days with Helen—right up to the space terminal, where Helen had been shot.

At that moment he was one of the most important and celebrated men in the empire, his name was being spread from world to world, and men would remember it as long as history was written; but he had been afraid to ask for the one piece of information that mattered most. *If she's dead, I don't want to know,* he thought, and sat unmoving, wondering at the tides of memory pounding at the walls of his consciouness, as though he had existed in this emotional matrix before, long ago, loving Helen in another life, losing her in another life. ...

"We'll touch down in less than a minute," Marshal Jennings said. "Are you ready for the ordeal?"

Tallon nodded. The space terminal was ballooning rapidly in the view screens. He could see the arrays of ships, the network of roads and crowded slideways, the space near the reception area that had been cleared for their landing. In another few seconds he made out the dark-suited figures of the official greeting party, which he had been told would include the Temporal Moderator himself. Cameramen were waiting to record his arrival for the benefit of the whole empire.

Suddenly, he recognized the pale oval of Helen's up-turned face amid the dark figures; and the turmoil in his mind subsided, leaving behind it a feeling of utter peacefulness, greater than he had ever expected to know.

"We'll have just enough room to land and nothing over," the lifeboat's pilot called over his shoulder. "This place is just as crowded as they say."

"A temporary phase," Tallon assured him. "Things are going to be different."

Helen's face was turned up toward his ship. But she could also have been looking beyond him to where the stars had begun to assemble in the evening sky. Toward— he recalled the old lines—that calm Sunday that goes on and on, when even lovers find their peace at last. The final line was: "And Earth is but a star, that once had shone," but that was something Helen and he and the rest of humanity did not have to think about.

The mother world would grow old some day, and become infertile; but by then her children would have grown up around her, tall and strong and fair. And they would be many.